His name is

PATRICK DAWLISH

He is a very large man, with vast shoulders that his well-cut suit cannot conceal. But for the broken nose, a legacy of an early battle in the boxing ring, he would be as handsome as he is massive . . .

He is always jumping in with both feet where the police fear to tread. And no thief, blackmailer or murderer ever comes up against a tougher, more resourceful, deadlier enemy than

PATRICK DAWLISH

A RABBLE OF REBELS, one of the Patrick Dawlish series, is by John Creasey writing as Gordon Ashe, of which there are now over forty titles and many have been published by Corgi Books.

Born in 1908, John Creasey has married three times, has three sons and has homes in both Wiltshire, Great Britain and in Arizona, USA where his books sell more than in any other country. Overall, John Creasey's books have sold nearly a hundred million copies and have been translated into 28 languages.

As well as an extensive traveller, he has a particular interest in politics and is the founder of *All Party Alliance*, which advocates a new system of government by the best candidates from all parties and independents. He has fought in five parliamentary by-elections for the movement.

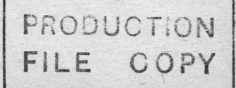

John Creasey
as Gordon Ashe

A Rabble of Rebels

CORGI BOOKS
A DIVISION OF TRANSWORLD PUBLISHERS LTD
A NATIONAL GENERAL COMPANY

A RABBLE OF REBELS

A CORGI BOOK 0 552 09226 6

Originally published in Great Britain
by John Long Limited

PRINTING HISTORY

John Long edition published 1971
Corgi edition published 1973

This book is set in Plantin 10 pt.

Corgi Books are published by Transworld Publishers Ltd.,
Cavendish House, 57–59 Uxbridge Road, Ealing,
London, W.5.

Made and printed in Great Britain by
Richard Clay (The Chaucer Press), Ltd., Bungay, Suffolk.

**NOTE: The Australian price appearing on the
back cover is the recommended retail price**

CONTENTS

A RABBLE OF REBELS

CHAPTER ONE

RABBLE

'There's going to be trouble,' said Gerald, in a husky voice.

'Let's get out,' urged Catherine, clutching his arm.

'Get *out*?' breathed Archie. 'If there's trouble, I want to be in the middle of it!'

He was the tallest of the three, sharp and eager-eyed, with clear-cut handsome features and a thrusting Roman nose. Catherine, a head shorter, was sturdy and full-figured, quite lovely in a dark-haired, olive-skinned way. Gerald, on her other side, was also sturdy, with a shock of stiff, very fair hair, overgrown from a crew-cut, stubby fair eyebrows, thick fair lashes.

They were at the northern edge of the sweeping lawns and great oaks and fir trees of the campus, with the main buildings half a mile away, the westering sun shining red and gold on the countless windows of the two tall towers, and on the connecting blocks about them.

Between these three students and the main buildings of the Mid-Cal University were hundreds of other students, all converging on the amphitheatre, legacy from Greeks and Romans in front of these modern reinforced concrete buildings. Young men and young women were disappearing over the edge all around the perimeter, as if they were jumping over a cliff. On the western side of the amphitheatre was the stage. Here, a dozen or so students had gathered about two flags which hung limply in the windless air.

Where Gerald and Catherine Lee were, with Archibald Nemaker, the ground was high, and they could see the campus as a great panorama, with the students approaching like tiny ant-like creatures, dressed in many colours. They were not straggling but walking purposefully, mostly from the east so that their faces were caught by the sun, which touched them all with radiance. Here was youth, walking towards tomorrow.

9

And as they dropped down into the stone bowels of the amphi-theatre the group on the stage placed microphones into posi-tion, rearranged tables and directed the crowd towards the empty rows of seats at the front.

'Gerald,' Catherine said, 'I really don't like it.'

'Let's go back,' Gerald urged. 'Archie . . .'

Archie's fine grey eyes were glistening, and his lips parted as if with uncontrollable excitement.

'We have to be there,' he said. 'We're in this with everyone else.'

'Archie . . .' Gerald began.

'Chicken?' demanded Archie, suddenly sneering. 'Okay, so you take Cathy to a drug store and have a milk shake, it'll match your liver.' He strengthened his stride, becoming one of the thrusting crowd, as purposeful as any. A small youth standing near by with a sheaf of newspapers under his arm called:

'Who'll buy a copy of *Student Action* for just twenty cents?'

Several students stopped to buy, none stopped to read, for they were eager to get to the amphitheatre.

The Lees still held back.

So did a few dozen others, as many youths as there were girls. As they hovered, others coming from behind pushed past them and a few jeered. Some of the reluctant ones quickened their pace with borrowed courage, others turned their backs on the still distant amphitheatre. Three were girls, all fair-haired, all very much alike, all lovely in their youth and freshness. They were, in fact, triplets.

More and more students were coming, now, from the north, where the Lees and Nemaker had come from. That was from the bay, where there were few homes; the city itself sprawled east, west and south, housing a million people of whom ten thousand came here, the newest of the mammoth extensions of the University of North and South California, known gener-ally as Mid-Cal.

A voice boomed from the loud-speakers.

'One-two-three-four-testing.'

'Testiiiing,' came the echo.

A man with a deeper voice called: 'There's plenty of room at the front. Come down, fellas, don't be nervous.'

'One-two-three-four-testing.'

'Testiiiing,' came the echo.

'Plenty of room . . .'

'*Student Action*—twenty cents,' a youth called.

Archie Nemaker had gone far ahead, and was lost to sight in the thickening crowd. Gerald, gripping his sister's arm, was moving determinedly in the other direction. No one else was near; the fainthearts had gone off the campus, those who had been urged forward had disappeared like Archie. The three blondes were a few yards ahead of Gerald and Catherine Lee when a knot of four youths appeared as if from nowhere and spread out across their path. They stood stationary, strangely menacing.

The three blondes stopped.

'Going places?' asked one of the youths in front of them.

The middle of the trio answered: 'We're going home.'

'Not yet you're not, baby.'

'Didn't you know there was a meeting on?' another youth asked.

'Sure,' put in a third. 'A Students for Action meeting. Don't you believe in student action?'

The three blondes seemed to hesitate, and then as if operated by the same switch, darted in different directions, long legs streaking, lithe bodies weaving. But the four youths were alert, and grabbed at swinging arms. One of the girls slipped, fell and cried out. Another found herself hugged tight. The third swung her right hand and caught her assailant a sharp blow on the cheek, darting away as she did so, but the fourth youth, standing clear until then, darted forward and grabbed her.

All of this took place in a few seconds.

No one except the Lees appeared to notice it. Most of the students in sight were hurrying towards the auditorium, the man announcing 'plenty of room' was now sending latecomers to the sides. The swarm of people had thinned and there was a two-deep fringe around the perimeter. A banner stretched out across the stage, black and red lettering on radiant white, reading: STUDENTS FOR ACTION.

There were sporadic outbursts of clapping, singing, shouting; the three girls held captive looked about them uncertainly.

'No one's leaving,' declared the fourth youth. 'Just turn round, honey-chillen, and . . .'

'*Run!*' whispered Gerald to his sister.

11

'*Gerald!*' breathed Catherine, in sudden anguish.

Her brother seemed to be propelled like a rocket from her side. He reached the youth holding the blonde close, pushed his wrist tight against the small of his back, and twisted. The youth gasped and staggered back.

'*Run!*' Gerald whispered into the ear of the girl he had freed.

She began to run; and Catherine was running, too, but looking back over her shoulder in anguish.

Gerald spun round towards the youth holding the other blonde by her wrist. The youth let her go.

'*Run!*' shouted Gerald.

The girl who had been tripped got to her feet, while all four of the attackers converged on Gerald Lee. As they came, he knew what they meant to do. Each had a hard, tough look and narrowed eyes. Catherine screamed and he heard the sound from afar off as he hurled himself forward, hoping to break the line, but his legs were hooked from under him. As he fell, the youth immediately in front of him kicked at his chin; his head seemed to break into pieces of bone and lacerated flesh as pain flashed through his body.

Catherine could not see exactly what happened. One moment Gerald's fair head showed above a pair of broad shoulders and the next it disappeared She turned, screaming, towards the four youths as they surrounded Gerald. She could see their legs and feet moving, knew they were kicking her brother. She reached one of them and clawed at his back but it made no difference at all, he went on kicking. The three blondes stopped running and one of them ran towards the seething group, while the others shouted:

'Help!'

'Please help!'

'Stop them!'

'Stop them!'

'They're killing him!'

Other young men, a few stragglers heading for the auditorium, a few with their backs towards it, stopped and watched. Two or three made half-hearted movements forward. One, quicker off the mark, had a girl beside him.

'Don't, Jim!' she cried.

The man faltered and stopped.

The two girls clawed and thumped at the heads and shoulders of the attackers, and Catherine suddenly began to kick. The man she kicked spun round and struck her across the face, sending her heavily to the ground.

In the distance, a police siren sounded; a banshee of warning.

The four men swung away from the huddled heap on the grass and ran in four directions. One student made an attempt to stop one of them, and was sent flying with a powerful hand-off. They raced towards a fringe of trees on the west, dark and soon lost against it. The blonde who had fought to help was now on her knees beside Catherine, who was struggling to get up and trying to see her brother as she did so. A man stepped between her and the battered body, to save her from the horror. Other girls and youths approached her while a few men moved slowly, with a fearful reluctance, towards Gerald Lee. He did not stir.

The siren wailed again.

A roar of sound came from the auditorium, and over the loud-speakers. A man with a piercing voice began to harangue the huge audience of over two thousand, while at least another thousand stood watching and listening, as if transfixed.

Among them was an older man than most, Leo Miraldi. He was known by a few who worked in the research laboratory where he was said to be taking a refresher course in crystallography. He was a tall man with sleek black hair and a high, pale forehead, a hooked nose and very sharp-cut lips. He wore a thin, off-white turtle-neck sweater and pale blue pants; and by chance he was only a few feet away from Archie Nemaker, who was listening with bated breath to the speaker.

'... So they give you a new building,' the high-pitched voice went on, 'and they make you pay for it ... So they give you a new building they tell you when to sit and when to stand and when to speak and when to button your mouth ...' The man on the platform paused, drawing in a breath which hissed over the loud-speaker system. 'So what are you going to do? Hey there! Let's see how well they've got you trained. *Sit!* You at the back there, *sit!*' And many of those standing on the perimeter squatted, and a few laughed. '*Stand!*' the man roared after, and instantly a few dozen in the middle of the auditorium rose up, and as the speaker roared again: '*Stand!*' the rest stood up with only a few exceptions.

13

Leo Miraldi stood.

Archibald Nemaker sat firmly where he was, his eyes glowing. 'Now speak, you slaves! Say "we want action".' There was a pause and then a girl behind him came forward, waving a baton, and sang into another microphone:

'*We—want—action!*'

From the packed masses men called out; here and there a girl's shriller voice could be heard.

'Action!'

'We want action!'

Dozens, *hundreds*, almost everyone in the audience, took up the phrase, putting emphasis on the last syllable.

'We—want—ac*tion.*'

'We—want ack*shun!*'

'We—want ack-*shun!*'

A few men and a few girls in the audience stayed in their seats and kept their mouths tightly closed. Leo Miraldi's eyes were on Archie Nemaker. Out of the blue came a stone, random-thrown, and it caught Archie on the temple, toppling him sideways against a man standing next to him. The man pushed him away. He bowed his head, and buried his face in his hands, obviously overcome by the pain. Another man called out in pain; a girl, also struck with a stone, collapsed.

The ginger-haired rabble-rouser raised both arms, the girl stopped chanting and the baton went still. Raggedly the chanting stopped, and in the near silence the speaker rasped:

'*Sit down!*'

They sat.

'Stand up!'

They stood.

The girl began to wave the baton but before she actually uttered a sound hundreds in the audience began to chant:

'We want ack-shun!'

'We want ack-shun!'

'*Student ack-shun!*'

There was some laughter; obviously to some it was a game, but to many it was in deadly earnest. Archie Nemaker stood up and tried to get away but it was impossible to force a way through. There was a huge swelling and some blood on his temple. A girl was stretched out at the foot of her seat, and a man was bending over her, dabbing at her forehead with a handkerchief.

The red-haired man was saying in his strident but strangely persuasive voice:

'We have to make the faculty understand that *we* know what is good for us ... We have to make the President know that we want a voice in the governing of the college ... It's our college, and we know what we want. Don't we?'

A few men and girls called out half-heartedly:

'Yes.'

'Try that again,' exhorted the speaker. 'We know what we want, don't we?'

'Yes!' came a roar. 'We know what we want!'

'And if we stick together we're going to get it,' the speaker said with overwhelming confidence. 'We want better food in the commissary ... We want an end to lectures where we have to sit and listen to pompous fools ... We want to participate ... Let me tell you there are hundreds of students in this college who know much more than the lecturers. What is the use today of what old men learned yesterday? ... This is the generation that can go to the moon but we're through with moonshine ... We want discussion with the professors, we want more professors and less discipline, we want, we want, we want...'

The words seemed to go on in ceaseless refrain. 'We want, we want, we want,' over and over again.

Two miles away, in the Hospital of the Good Samaritan, Gerald Lee lay between life and death. Catherine, badly bruised, sat by his side. His parents were flying up from a little town near Escondido in Southern California, the police were questioning eye-witnesses and learning very little, the four youths who had carried out the savage attack had disappeared without trace.

And police, armed with night-sticks and tear-gas pistols, were quietly surrounding the campus grounds.

CHAPTER TWO

RABBLE-ROUSER

Leo Miraldi watched and listened, fascinated. The red-haired man on the platform was now moving to and fro, rather like a pop-singer. Watching the continuous opening and closing of his mouth, it was possible to imagine that he was singing. But he was not; he was reciting. There was a curious rhythm about the way his words were uttered, and that rhythm held the crowd. They swayed to it. Not deeply, just a slight swaying of the body as if they were subconsciously keeping time. And in the background, very faint, was music; primitive music; the drums which might be tom-toms beating out a message.

'We need a voice in the affairs of the college ... and we shall have that voice.

'We need new men, new ideas, new methods of teaching ... and we shall have new men, new ideas, new methods.

'We need better food and cheaper food ... and we shall have better food and cheaper food.

'We need more space.

'We need more books.

'We need ... we need ... we need ...

'We want ... we want ... we want ...

'We shall have ...

'We shall have ... '

The voice, the distant sound of drums, the warmth of the evening, all seemed to combine to hypnotise the thousands who sat and swayed and stood and swayed. Miraldi, looking about him occasionally but most of the time staring at the orator as if he too were enthralled, saw others, even more watchful. And he began to take careful note. These others were mostly youths, although a few were girls. They seemed to sit equidistant from one another. Miraldi counted heads away from the youngster with an incipient bald patch. Twenty heads, six-

16

teen male, four female, to the right and there was another of these watchful individuals. Twenty heads to the left ... twenty heads forward. He checked with four of the youths who were watching the audience more than they were watching the orator. So each of those he had noticed kept about thirty people under surveillance.

He was under observation from behind, no doubt.

As the noise from the drums became louder and the rhythm faster, the words spilled more quickly from the orator's pale lips.

'We need a voice and we shall have a voice.

'We need new ideas and we shall have new ideas.

'We need new methods and we shall have new methods ...' He paused and his clenched right hand beat time to the drums ... 'and we shall fight any who get in our way.' Softly, softly, he repeated: 'We shall fight any who get in our way ... we shall *fight, fight, fight.*'

He stopped: and almost every eye was turned towards him. Almost, but not all; not those of people who were glancing about them, the watching girls and youths—one of whom, Miraldi reminded himself, was watching him. *Why?* They were spies, of course, looking out for any who did not fall beneath this man's spell. The spell worked almost as if it were a drug; the speaker was now standing rigid, eyes turned slightly upwards as if invoking some power in the skies.

Very softly, but with that harsh, near-strident voice, he began again:

'Do you know what they did in Los Angeles? Do you know what they did in San Francisco? Do you know what they did in Cleveland, Ohio? Do you know what they did in Richmond, Virginney? ... Do you know? ... Then I will tell you. *They called out the cops.*'

'Shame!' a man screamed back.

'The bastard cops!' another yelled.

'Shame, shame, shame—shame—shame!'

'That's right on the nose,' the speaker approved, more loudly, more viciously. 'We know what we want, we mean to get what we want, and no cops are going to stop us. We've got guns and we know how to use them.'

Someone bellowed: 'Cops!'

Another shouted: 'The cops are here.'

'Don't let them stop us,' cried the ginger-haired man, and

17

now he seemed to be dancing with fury. And he drew a pistol from his pocket and brandished it around, while the drumbeats grew still louder. 'Don't let them stop us!'

'*Cops!*' several men called at once.

And many of the students drew revolvers and many more drew knives, while some held rocks and broken bottles, weapons and missiles of all kinds.

'*Sit in!*' cried the ginger-haired man. 'Storm the buildings! Sit in! Sit in!'

Suddenly all the men and women whom Miraldi had noticed were on their feet, yelling: 'Sit in! Strike! Take the buildings, take the buildings!' And as they shouted and began to thrust their way towards the top, others turned and climbed and pushed, while those who had been standing on the rim of the amphitheatre were thrust back, some moving as if eagerly, some with evident reluctance. Whether eager or reluctant they went forward in a solid phalanx towards the new buildings, where the windows still reflected a golden sun, dazzling enough to blind them to the sight of the police, approaching in a wide spaced cordon.

Quite suddenly, men at the front of the students began to run; and others followed until it was like a stampede of savage animals, footsteps thundering on the hard turf as they hurtled towards the buildings. From the right and the left the police came, more stolidly, almost as if they did not know what they should do. Some began to run towards the wings of the stampeding students, but they were too late. The leaders, like trained storm-troopers, raced up the wide marble steps and through the main doors. Two older men stood at a balcony above the doors, peering down as if in horror. The quiet halls and rooms and passages suddenly crackled with noise; the rattle of steel-tipped shoes. Students spread into the wings of the building, bursting into lecture rooms, into laboratories, into libraries, into private studies. And as they tore about the college and the sharp noise of steel on stone floors grew louder, voices rose, too, and here was Bedlam.

Outside, thousands of the students hung back, and all of them were harangued by others, behind them. And the police, outnumbered twenty or thirty to one, hesitated in fatal apprehension. Suddenly bottles flew; and rocks; and cans: and at a flick of a knife there was pandemonium outside the university as well as in.

18

In the Hospital of the Good Samaritan, Gerald Lee died while his sister watched the bruised and battered face.

The three blondes wept as Catherine wept.

They were led out of the ward and to the quiet lawns some distance from the campus. A sound as of roaring came from a long way off, but they did not know and could not see. Two ambulances drew up and injured youths were helped down from them. Soon rumours began to spread.

'There's a riot at the campus.'

'Shooting.'

'The students have taken over the buildings.'

'There's a riot ... take-over ... the police have charged ... tear gas.'

'Petrol bombs.'

Fast upon the rumours came the newspapermen and the television teams. Helicopters flew overhead, taking picture after picture of the struggling, seething mass below. In small groups the police lined up to keep the students at bay and time and time again knots of teenagers, at least a quarter of them girls, flung themselves at the police, or stood back and hurled rocks and broken bottles, forcing the use of tear gas. But there was the wind. It blew gently from the ocean towards the town, and the concentration of gas on the campus, even inside the college buildings, was comparatively low. Students, tears streaming from their eyes, could nevertheless see; and the savagery with which they broke up the police cordons in order to get into the building appalled the police leaders.

The waves of the gas reached first the residential part of the city, the expensive homes of the wealthy; creeping insidiously onward to the broad Main Street, into the shops and homes, drug stores and bottle stores. Onward then, borne on the gentle wind, to the poorer parts of the town, the small, crowded streets where the Mexican-Americans lived with their huge families. It set the children crying; the babies too, and soon the men and women.

A policeman, getting out of his air-conditioned car, saw two children reeling away from each other, crying and screaming. He, too, felt the bite of the gas, and raised an alarm. Further use of gas was stopped, but all that was there rolled sluggishly on.

The campus area, beginning to clear, revealed a terrifying picture.

19

Dozens of police were seen to be badly injured. Hundreds of students lay about, felled by rocks, knives, bullets and broken bottles. Clothes, shoes, sandals, were strewn about everywhere, with the missiles which had done so much harm. There were gas pistols and thousands of spent cartridges against the litter of torn copies of *Student Action*. There were people limping and crawling towards hoped-for help, and others being carried or dragged.

Youths and girls were crying or groaning from the pain of injury, from rage and mortification. More gritted their teeth as they limped away from the scene. A crowd of five or six hundred gathered outside the main entrance, now barred and barricaded by the police with advance units of the National Guard already on the way. Inside were a thousand students rampaging through passages and rooms.

On the second floor, in his study, the Principal stood at the window with two of his colleagues. On the main desk was a microphone through which he could talk to everyone inside and, by a public address system, to huge assemblies outside. Some of the students were looking up at the window, some touched their friends and pointed, so that more and more looked towards this man.

One of those with him, stocky Daniel Armour, with his pebble-lensed glasses and his deeply lined face, joined him at the window.

'What are you going to do, Joe?' he asked. 'You've got to do something.'

Professor Joseph Connell, tall, grey-haired, gentle-faced, with heavy-lidded grey eyes, looked down at him.

'I can't believe it's happened,' he said brokenly. 'I just can't believe it.'

'We've got the evidence of our eyes,' retorted Armour drily. 'Sending for the police didn't work, so you've got to try something else.'

'I had no idea, no idea at all, that they had such grievances.' Connell's voice was laden with self-reproach.

'Who said they've grievances?' Philip Pardoe, deputy Administrator, dark-haired, bold-eyed, with sloping shoulders somehow emphasised by his beautifully tailored pearl-grey suit, moved to join the others at the window. As he opened his mouth to go on there was a thunderous roar from the crowd outside. Hundreds were now looking up at the window, a few

20

were shaking fists. Suddenly there was a clatter, then a thud-ding of feet and a roar as of an avalanche; students had broken down the passage door leading to these administration offices.

'Oh my God!' breathed Connell.

'They don't have any grievances,' Pardoe went on. 'They're a rabble of rebels, no more, no less. Kalta is a trained rabble-rouser, and he must have a hundred helping him.'

'Joe,' said Armour, 'you'll have to talk to them.'

'Talking won't do any good,' Pardoe said coldly. 'They need a few days in the pen to cool off.'

The noise drew nearer, more fearsome. There was no cer-tainty that the students in the passage were coming to break in here, but it seemed inevitable. Connell's long, pale, delicate fingers spread out and pressed on the square-topped desk be-hind him—and a tomato smashed against the window, the juicy flesh flowing down the window-pane like fresh-spilled blood.

Quite suddenly, Connell spun round.

There was a heavy bang on the door from the passage, divided by an ante-room from this office.

Connell picked up the microphone, dropped into his padded armchair, and flicked on the switch which was marked: *All Loud-speakers*. He gulped; but suddenly he stopped trem-bling, and his voice came clear and strong.

'Quiet, please. This is Professor Connell.'

There was a huge cheer from outside, on a jeering note, and more fruit was thrown, more juice flowed down the glass.

'I will receive a deputation of five, in my office, when the rest of the building is cleared,' he said firmly. Both Armour and Pardoe looked at him in astonishment, Armour with ob-vious admiration. 'You may name your delegates and I will pay close attention to any grievances they express. Now, please. Clear the college building. And once outside, withdraw to a reasonable distance. If those of you now on the campus immediately outside this office move back a hundred yards— no, fifty yards will suffice—then you will not incite the police or the National Guard.' There was another, more subdued cheer, with less jeering, as he paused. His voice was even more incisive as he went on: 'I presume the captain in charge of the police is within earshot. Captain, will you be good enough to make a passage at the front of the building, enabling those who are inside to walk out without hindrance . . . Thank you.'

He switched off, and immediately he began to tremble again. His forehead, upper lip and neck were covered with a film of perspiration. Armour put a hand on his shoulder.

'That was great, Joe—just great, wasn't it, Philip?'

'It was good,' agreed Pardoe. 'But it won't succeed. The rabble's inside and won't go now. And look—they're beginning to argue among themselves.' He was close to the window, watching. 'A couple have started fighting.' He turned to face the quivering president, and his voice had a whip-like sharpness. 'This rabble has to be cleared out by the police or by the National Guard. They won't listen to reason, and if you don't get them out quickly they'll take over. As they did in Mexico City, in Paris and the London School of Economics.' He paused. Get them *out*, Joe. Tell the police that the situation is out of hand.'

Across the last word came a thunderous banging at the passage door, a rending sound, as if the door was down. Outside, the crowd was breaking up into small groups, mostly arguing and haranguing, but here and there sniffling. Connell stretched out for the microphone again. This time the metamorphosis was not so complete, his voice trembled over some words.

'This is Professor Connell. I promise—I p-promise you I will meet five delegates and—and—listen to your grievances if you will com-comport yourselves with dignity and intelligence.'

A stone crashed through the window.

Thudding of feet rumbled across the ante-room and someone banged on the study door.

'Open up!' cried a man, undoubtedly the ginger-haired Kalta. 'We want to talk to you.'

'That's Kalta,' Armour said.

'I told you so,' put in Pardoe. 'Our only hope is with the National Guard.'

There was a heavy thudding on the door, and it began to open.

Outside there came a chant.

'We want ack-shun. *Student* ack-shun!'

CHAPTER THREE

NEW YORK

Across the nation, on radio and television, on huge headlines in the newspapers and by word of mouth, news of the latest student outbreak flashed minute by minute, and flashed almost as quickly across the world. Most people read or heard of it with a kind of resignation. *God knows what these yobs will get up to, these days.* Others heard with a sense of increasing alarm. *There's hell in the young people; what will happen if they take over governments?* Others again, by far a minority, said viciously or bitterly: *It's the Communists, the Reds. Russia's behind this:* and these believed what they said to be true.

The President was worried ... The leaders of the Department of Education were acutely disappointed for they had made so many concessions to students, collaborating with State universities to create near ideal conditions. The Federal Bureau of Investigation, with its evergreen director, was angry and worried. So were educational and police authorities in all the forty-eight mainland states of the United States of America.

And in New York, Assistant Commissioner Randy Patton was worried, for there were rumours of similar trouble brewing at New Columbia, the new university in New York City, far north in Manhattan and on the banks of the Hudson River. Built as an overflow from Columbia, it had not been treated as an extension, but projected, constructed and opened with a great fanfare, only two years before. For over a year, its students had seemed almost overwhelmed by the air-conditioned glass palaces, the exceptional facilities offered in every phase of the university's activities: but there had been some isolated outbursts of revolt in the past few months; protests at the discipline of attending lectures; of a 'curfew' at midnight; at supervision between the male and the female sleeping quarters.

23

These had been growing. Patton, who had two lieutenants and a sergeant on the staff of New Columbia, was informed of trouble long before it began. So far, there was no reason to take action, but the causes for anxiety quickened, and now that Bentham North and Mid-Cal college had erupted, trouble might flash to the tinder-dry conditions at New Columbia.

Patton was in his office, in the old police headquarters in downtown New York: alone. A television set flickered its pale pictures of the scenes at Mid-Cal. The commentator was saying:

'At least one student, Gerald Crowhurst Lee, aged 21, has died as a result of the riots. Sixty-three students, twenty-four policemen and eleven National Guardsmen have been treated in hospital. The condition of eleven students and four policemen is grave. The campus, landscaped with great pride only a year ago, looks like a battlefield.' Almost casually, the commentator went on: 'The Principal, Professor Joseph Connell, with the Assistant Administrator and one member of the faculty, are being held prisoners in the college offices.' A student carrying a sheaf of slim-looking newspapers was shouting: '*Student Action*, who'll buy *Student Action*? Read all about it in *Student Action*.' The camera caught the wild look in the *Student Action* seller's eyes; a long-haired, ascetic-looking youth who held the newspaper up to his chin as the camera focused on him.

A telephone on Patton's desk rang.

He saw pictures of a man at the window of the offices, heard the names enunciated and then lifted the receiver: the television was turned low so that he could hear what was said on the telephone.

'Patton,' he announced.

'Commissioner, there is a call for you from London,' Headquarters operator said.

'London!' Patton ejaculated, and his heavy-lidded eyes became huge. He had a vivid mental picture of a face of a man with cornflower blue eyes and a broken nose—a London policeman named Patrick Dawlish. 'Is it from Mr. Dawlish?'

'That's right, sir '

'I'll talk to him!' Patton said quickly.

'Hold on, please.'

He held on, thoughts flashing through his mind. Of the huge Dawlish, Deputy Assistant Commissioner of the Metropolitan

Police in London; of the time when they had last met at a gathering of policemen from all over the world. Dawlish was the British delegate to a conference of police forces from the world; he, Patton, had long been the delegate from New York and Eastern United States. Patton remembered, with sharp pain, his dead wife, who had first betrayed him as a police officer and then thrown herself out of the window of Dawlish's flat, atop one of the tallest buildings in London.

He thought of his daughter, who had so nearly died because of her mother's betrayal of police secrets.

There were noises on the line; a whining and squeaking, until Dawlish's deep voice sounded as if he were close by.

'Randy?'

'Pat, it's good to hear you!'

'How are you?' Dawlish sounded as if the answer really mattered.

'I'm fine, Pat.'

'Worried but fine,' said Dawlish, unexpectedly.

'What's that?'

'I suggested you were worried but bearing up well!'

Patton found himself chuckling; one of his most vivid memories of Dawlish was the way the Englishman could make him laugh in almost any situation. If there were a funny side, Dawlish would find it.

'What am I worried about?' inquired Patton.

'New Columbia, now that the top's blown off at Mid-California,' Dawlish answered, and the note of laughter faded from his voice. 'How bad are things, Randy?'

'They are very bad indeed,' answered Patton.

He spoke slowly, so as to give himself time to think. Why was Dawlish so interested in the new universities? What did he know about New Columbia? (The world knew now, of course, of the revolt at Mid-California.)

'I was afraid so,' Dawlish said. 'There's been a quiet spell everywhere, but it looks as if Mid-Cal and New Columbia are flashpoints for trouble in a lot of other places.'

Patton grunted: 'Do you mean that?' Suddenly, appalled, he had a mental picture of the fighting on the campus at the Mid-Cal flare-up, saw a squad of Civil Guard rush towards a strongly packed group of students.

'World-wide,' Dawlish said.

'Good God!' exclaimed Patton.

25

'I've been talking to Van Woeldon,' Dawlish said. Van Woeldon was a Dutchman who had become the director of the police conference, which was in constant session. Every now and again a crime or series of crimes had world-wide repercussions and special sessions of the conference were called at short notice. 'He's going to call a special session as soon as possible.'

'On campus troubles?' demanded Patton.

'Officially on drug peddling; no one will be surprised about that,' said Dawlish. 'Actually, on campus trouble. Can you come?'

'I guess so,' Patton said. 'I'll have to get approval from on high, but—sure, I can come. They won't stop me. Where? London?'

'That's what I want to talk to you about,' said Dawlish. 'New world or old world?'

'Pat,' said Patton, heavily, 'I don't think this is the right country for it at this time. There would be a lot of resentment if it went round that the conference was coming to put our colleges right. Don't hold this one in the U.S.A. That's a considered opinion.'

'Then it might be London, or Paris,' Dawlish mused. 'Possibly Frankfurt, there hasn't been any trouble there, no one could think we were trying to put the West German house in order.'

'Brussels?' suggested Patton, and added briskly: 'Forget it! Wherever you hold the session, I'll be there, but Pat ...' He paused.

'Yes?'

'How widespread are the troubles?' asked Patton.

'There are rumours of coming outbreaks in Sydney, New South Wales, Copenhagen, New Delhi, Tokyo, Buenos Aires, Mexico City, Cairo and, believe it or not, Russia!' Dawlish answered.

'Good God!' ejaculated Patton again.

'That is probably what the Russians themselves think,' Dawlish said, the quirk of humour showing itself. 'What we want is an up-to-the-minute report from all countries about their university situations. Can you get one quickly?'

'I've a man on his way here from Mid-Cal,' Patton interrupted. 'He's working for the F.B.I. and seconded to me and Mid-Cal. All our universities are closely watched. I'll bring more reports than the conference can handle.'

'That will be the day,' Dawlish retorted lightly.

'What are you really asking for?' asked Patton. 'Connecting links? Pieces in a puzzle?'

'We're looking for a pattern,' Dawlish said. 'Sorry.'

'These puns.' Patton retorted scornfully. 'Is that all?'

'What we particularly want to find out is whether any campus troubles develop in the same way ... Whether the rabble-rousers involved are indigenous, so to speak, or imported. Is there a local training college for rabble-rousers; in short, or an international one.'

'I can tell you this,' said Patton. 'Nine F.B.I. men out of ten will tell you it's caused by the Reds.'

'That's what we have to find out,' retorted Dawlish. 'The question is ...'

'Yes?'

'Would the Reds start trouble at Moscow University?' demanded Dawlish. 'There's talk of a major revolt over there.'

Patton grunted. 'The trans-Siberian railroad is still open, isn't it?'

Dawlish laughed, but did not really seem amused.

'I'll tell you where the session is going to be as soon as it's decided.'

'Sure, Pat. And thanks for calling.' In a sharp voice, as if in afterthought, Patton added: 'How is Felicity?'

Felicity was Dawlish's wife. And Felicity had tried so hard to help his, Patton's, wife; and to help Patton and his daughter during those tragic days in London. The pain, so great then, so unbearable, was nearly as hurtful now.

'She's fine,' Dawlish answered. 'And Dodie?'

Dodie was Patton's daughter.

'Still pining for your policemen,' answered Patton. 'Gordon Scott.'

'Can you bring her over?' suggested Dawlish.

'Not a chance in a million,' answered Patton. 'She's majoring in political science and wants out this year. Did you know she and Gordon write to each other at least once a week?'

'I'd no idea.' After a pause, Dawlish went on in a bright voice: 'We'll have to get them together somehow. Give her my love.'

'Surely,' promised Patton.

'There's one other thing,' Dawlish said.

'Name it,' responded Patton.

'One common factor that we've found in many countries is the student newspaper, *Student Action*,' Dawlish told him. 'Is it common with you?'

'There's one on every campus,' Patton told him. He could 'see' the ascetic face of the youth who had been held in focus in the television camera a few minutes ago. 'There always has been. What's so special about them?'

'Every university started with its own, printed on the campus or by a local printer,' Dawlish said, 'but we've found that only the outside pages are local now. The inside pages are photolitho'd. They give world news, as they call it, much of it inflammatory and seditious stuff. And the local columns are slanted. It looks as if each campus has at least one very clever write-up man, who uses the *Student Action* to inflame local opinion, while the other pages imply that the whole world is bitterly anti-youth. Will you check as many as you can on your side?'

'You bet I will,' Patton promised.

He rang off, and for a few minutes sat reflecting on *Student Action*. But soon his thoughts drifted to Dodie, young Scott and the wreckage of his own marriage, broken in spirit long before the disaster in London. Slowly the pictures on the screen drew his thoughts away from gloomy memories. Now and again commercials introduced a note of banality into the riot scenes, but in one way they showed them up in their full horror.

His telephone bell rang again.

'Patton,' he answered, forcing himself to sound brisk.

'Commissioner, this is Leo Miraldi,' a man announced laconically. 'I'm at San Francisco airport, and I'm booked on TWA Flight 1071 due at Kennedy at twelve-fifty, Eastern Standard time. Will you want to see me as soon as I arrive, or in the morning.'

'As soon as you arrive,' Patton answered promptly. 'If I'm not at Kennedy myself to meet you, I'll have a car waiting. Do what the driver tells you, that'll be okay.'

He hung up, stood up and went to the television, turning it off. The office seemed very quiet. It was now seven-thirty; he had good time for dinner, and to check over his reports from New Columbia. He put in his request for a visit to Europe, and went down in the big elevator. Coming up one side of the central staircase when he reached the main floor was a group

28

of Negroes and Costa Ricans, handcuffed in couples; they looked shame-faced. On the other side was a handsome youth with his collar and tie twisted round his neck, a savage expression in his eyes: two plainclothes detectives held him tightly. At the entrance to the offices, a woman was arguing with the sergeant on duty.

'He's my husband, I want to see him. I've got a right to see him.'

Patton went out, down the stone steps and past the two great lions, on to cobbled streets along which cars and taxis, trucks and people rumbled or clattered constantly. He walked for twenty minutes with long strides, a man nearly six feet tall, very broad but lean, although his face held fleshiness and at forty-five he had quite a jowl. He looked pale as if he needed a rest, mostly in the sun. He was on Lexington Avenue with traffic hurtling past in its one-way torrent when he flagged down a taxi.

'Eighty-first at Riverside,' he said.

The driver took him to Sixth Avenue—the Avenue of the Americas, the emblems on the lamp-posts declared. Here could be seen old brown-stone shops, huge areas ready for demolition, the tall modern starkness of the *Time and Life* building and the strange obscurity of the New York Hilton. Soon Sixth debouched on to Central Park South. His driver skirted a horse-drawn cab festooned with artificial flowers, the top hatted driver sitting high above the slow rise and fall of his horse's haunches. Then through Central Park, a blend of grass and trees and dogs and people, the atmosphere one of relaxation and pleasure. He reflected how, at the northern end of the park, it was hardly safe to walk alone even in broad daylight.

'What the hell *is* happening to the world?' he asked aloud.

Over on the west, standing and waiting at some traffic lights, was a crocodile of young people, all colours, all ages from early to late teens. They looked clean and scrubbed and polished. And eager. Where they were going he had no idea, but sight of them lifted his heart momentarily. He took two dollars from his clip as the cab slowed down at the corner of 81st Street at Riverside Drive. Here, traffic was thin, parked cars seemed to have stood at the kerbs forever. Winding Riverside Drive, with its gardens, stretched far in each direction. The elevated section of the Henry Hudson Parkway carved the river in two, and cars raced along it as if their drivers were eager to reach eternity.

A little old woman was tugging at a rebellious King Charles spaniel as Patton turned into the big old house where he had an apartment. He had only been here a year and as yet was not at home with it. The elevator crawled upwards but at last he was on the eighth floor and inside his flat. The view across the busy Hudson was a constant attraction, and the view from a corner window showed him the George Washington Bridge spanning the river in slender symmetry, the new carriage-way, 'Martha', beneath.

He could see, through gaps in trees, the windows and the roof of New Columbia.

Aloud, he said again: 'What the hell *is* happening?'

Then he recalled Dawlish's almost sombre talk of threatened or at least expected trouble in so many countries, even behind the Iron Curtain. He mixed himself a Martini, sipped it as he stood by the window, then went to the refrigerator; this was a night for a home-cooked hamburger and coffee. Jacket off, he spent fifteen minutes at the electric stove, then sat, as the percolator bubbled and popped, eating, glooming. He was nearly through when the telephone bell rang.

'This is a night for trouble,' he muttered, stretching forward for the wall telephone. 'Hallo. Randy Patton.'

'Will Commissioner Randolph Patton take a call collect from Boulder, Colorado?' the operator asked.

Flash thoughts sliced through his mind as he said: 'Surely.' This was Dodie, who was at Boulder University. She wouldn't call him unless it were an emergency. She had a sense of shame of calling collect, and had another month at the university before sitting for her degree. What could be the matter at such a time? Her clear, firm voice sounded at last.

'Daddy, are you there?'

'Sure, honey. It's good to hear you.'

'Daddy,' she repeated hurriedly. 'I haven't time to explain now but I—I'm in trouble. *Serious* trouble. There's a fast flight out of Denver at ten-fifteen, it reaches Kennedy at two-fifty. Flight 8012. Could you meet me at Kennedy? Could you, *please*?'

30

CHAPTER FOUR

TROUBLE

'She's going to have a baby,' Patton said in a clear, flat voice. 'What else can it be if she wouldn't talk over the telephone?' He poured out another cup of coffee, added cream and carried it to the living room, where his bag was by the side of a big armchair. Coffee spilled in his saucer as he sat down, and he poured it into the cup. 'My God!' he exclaimed. 'She's pregnant '

He thought of Gordon Scott.

He reminded himself that he was to send for or meet Miraldi at Kennedy. The obvious thing to do was go and meet the agent and take him to a bar or a coffee shop while they waited for Dodie's flight. They were on the same line so at the same terminal building. He put his case on an upright chair, opened it and began to study the information he had collected about the student troubles. There was a complete list of universities in the United States where there had been riots or trouble of some kind. A brief summary prepared by a Homicide Squad lieutenant who had been on the team investigating a murder at Harvard helped. At all the universities and university colleges covered, there had been trouble. Only a few colleges, all connected with religious bodies, had been free from it.

The religious would say that good would out; or else that it was the will of God.

The sceptics would say it was lack of courage, or meek acceptance of their lot.

Whatever the reason, the facts were simple: for three years ending last fall disturbances had been on a grand scale. They had gradually lessened this year, but only slightly. The outbreak at Mid-Cal and the threatened one at New Columbia were changing this trend. He read some of the stated causes: in the immediate past these had mostly been anti-Vietnam,

Cambodia, anti-nuclear weapons or Civil Rights. Some demonstrations had involved thousands, like the trouble at Berkeley in Northern California, some only a few hundred.

By the time Patton had soaked himself in the information it was nearly time to leave for Kennedy Airport. He needed at least an hour, because after-theatre traffic could be very heavy. He went down to his parked green Oldsmobile, in a lot near by, and drove across town to the Roosevelt Parkway. The lights on the bridges spanning the East River to Queens and Brooklyn had a glittering brightness in the clear, still night. He took the Triboro Bridge, then drove along the parkways towards the airport. Green and red lights on aircraft vied with the stars. He was at the magnificent main hall of the TWA terminal at twenty-thirty, checked that Miraldi's flight was on time, checked that Dodie's had left on time and paced the great hall impatiently until it was time to go along to the gate where the flight from Los Angeles was due to arrive.

The flight's arrival was announced to the minute; very soon Miraldi would appear, with his rather loping walk and almost shy manner. Passengers arrived, were reunited with friends and families, couples walked off, preoccupied with themselves, a girl in her twenties, alone, was obviously pregnant, as obviously self-conscious.

Like Dodie?

The passengers dwindled to a few scattered individuals, but there was no Miraldi.

'Will you have a drink, sir?' the stewardess asked Miraldi.
'Sure,' he accepted. 'Make it a bourbon and water.'
'On the rocks?'
'Yes, please.'

She gave him his drink, and went on. He sipped, watched the dozens of heads in front of him, the ceaseless to and froing of passengers along the gangway, the busy stewards and hostesses, the muted clatter of the food trays. He made some notes about what he was to tell Patton; he liked to have notes, not only as aids to his memory, but as a basis for written reports to come. He sketched a section of the auditorium and made dots for the heads of students, circles round the dots for the obvious watchers, spies. He wondered, a little amusedly, which student had been watching him. A youth coming back from the toilet jogged his arm as he picked up a copy of the Mid-Cal edition of *Student Action*. The radio buzzed and a voice sounded.

'*Good evening, ladies and gentlemen, this is Captain Osborne. I hope you're all having a good flight with TWA. Out on the left side, you can see the northern edge of the Grand Canyon ... We are cruising at 30,000 feet, and the weather is clear all the way to New York, you can count on being on time. I'll let you know if there are any changes.*'

Miraldi, in common with all but the most hardened travellers, looked out of the left-side window, craning his neck. Someone jogged his elbow again and muttered: 'Sorry.' He did not look round: there was such fascination in the enormous canyon, the mountains below the level of the great plateau of Northern Arizona. At last, it fell from sight. He turned back in his seat, picked up his glass, and tossed the rest of the drink down. It was then that he saw the youth with the pinched nostrils and the long, spade-shaped chin; a youth he had seen when he had left the amphitheatre.

His heart seemed to smash at his ribs, the onslaught of fear was so great. For the youth was grinning at him, slyly, triumphantly.

A moment later, Miraldi began to choke.

A moment later still, he felt a sharp, stabbing pain in his head.

There was time only for another fleeting moment of alarm before he blacked out. He had hardly time to realise that he was dying.

The hostess came along to take his glass; came later to put down his tray for dinner. She gave up trying to wake him—passengers who were dead to the world were not uncommon. But when he was still 'sleeping' after the meal, having touched nothing, she was puzzled. Soon, she was alarmed and went up to report to the flight deck.

The tired-looking man left in charge of the gate looked at Patton with patient resignation. Here was the man who had left a brief-case or wallet or book or some such thing on the aircraft. He started up in respectful surprise when Patton showed him his badge.

'Help you, sir?'

'Do you have a passenger list of Flight 1071?'

'No, sir. It's gone to the main office.'

'Check if there was a passenger named Miraldi on it,'

Patton ordered. 'A male passenger.'

'*M-Miraldi!*' exclaimed the clerk, and the way he spoke sent a shaft of alarm through Patton.

'That's right,' he made himself say calmly. 'What do you know about him?'

'He—he died, sir. He was taken off in an ambulance, he didn't come through the gate. He . . .' The clerk broke off. 'I'm sorry, sir.'

'Call the airport police and tell them I'm on my way,' Patton ordered, and swung round, striding back to the main hall and the airport police. By the time he reached a small group of men in the Security Office in the TWA terminal, it was twenty-five past twelve. He was recognised by a tall, fair-haired Swede, named Carlsen, who came across the office, with its green-coloured steel furniture, hand outstretched.

'Are you after Miraldi, Commissioner?'

'Yes. *Is* he dead?' Patton could still hardly believe it.

'Sure he is,' Carlsen told him. 'He's been dead for over three hours. He's on the way to the City Hospital in an ambulance. You missed him by five minutes.' Carlsen talked as if the corpse had been responsible for its own movements. 'Did you come to meet him, Commissioner?'

'Yes. And now I need to call my office.' Patton picked up the telephone which the lieutenant indicated, dialled and talked at the same time. 'I want a passenger list from that flight. I want all the crew held in the terminal, if any have left I want them brought back . . . How soon can you fix it?' His glare at the lieutenant was almost as cold as his manner was demanding. Then a voice sounded at the other end of the line. 'Homicide . . . Who's in charge? . . . Okay, put me through to him.' He glared at the airport policeman. 'How soon can I have that passenger list?'

'I've sent for it, Commissioner.'

'Hurry it up.' Patton's voice was terse. 'The crew?'

'I've sent out a call. Two of them may have left the airport.'

'Find out how they went, car, cab or bus, and have them brought back . . . Caleb.' Now he was talking on the telephone. 'Randy. I want the passengers in TWA Flight 1071 from L.A. to Kennedy traced quicker than you can say fire. A copy of the list will be on teletype to you in a few minutes, have someone stand by. I'm at Kennedy, TWA Building, keep me informed as you trace them one by one. Okay?'

34

The man Caleb answered almost breathlessly: 'Okay.'

'Don't lose a minute.' He put down the receiver with deceptive gentleness, and asked the Scandinavian: 'Lieutenant, was anything found on or near Miraldi?'

'Found?'

'In his pockets, case, on his seat, the floor . . .'

'He was taken away with his clothes on, so . . .'

'Do you know the number of the hospital?'

'I can get it for you.'

'Thanks. Have someone stop the garbage from that flight, we need to go through it.' He hardly paused when a man said: 'I'll fix it,' and went out, but careered on: 'What precinct is the hospital—okay, okay, I remember. Get me the hospital, I want to talk to Queens Number 5 Precinct.' Already he was dialling, and already Carlsen was on the other instrument. Patton seemed oblivious of the staring faces, and his voice shot outwards as if from a machine-gun. 'Captain Liducci? . . . Commissioner Patton.' He sat back and pushed his hair from his forehead and went on with a half-smile: 'Do you have some water?'

'*Water!*' ejaculated Carlsen, and a man almost jumped towards a water container with some Dixie cups in a wall fastening.

'Captain Liducci? . . . A man named Miraldi was taken from Flight 1071 TWA, believed dead,' said Patton. 'I want everything found in his pockets and a thorough laboratory check on his clothes and an autopsy, *quick* . . . Yes . . . Yes, Miraldi . . . If the newspapers ask questions you don't know a damned thing. Thanks . . . I'll be at TWA terminal building, Kennedy . . . Thanks.' He rang off, took a paper cup from the other man's hand, sipped, leaned back and looked up at Carlsen. Almost as soon as he did so, the door opened and a girl in the smart TWA uniform came in, carrying a sheaf of papers.

'Someone wants the passenger list on Flight 1071,' she said.

'Here,' called Carlsen.

'Were you on the flight?' asked Patton.

'Yes,' the girl answered. 'I was just going off duty when a standby call came.'

'My fault,' Patton said, and showed his badge. 'I need to know everything you can tell me about that flight, and especially about anyone who sat near or passed close to Mr. Miraldi.'

'Almost everybody passed him,' she answered at once. She

35

had a nice skin, pleasant blue eyes, rather thin lips. 'He had an outside seat, and anyone who went to the toilets passed him at least twice.'

Patton was glancing down the passenger list.

'Who last saw him awake?' he asked.

'I gave him a bourbon and water on the rocks,' she said, and gave a little shudder. 'I may have been the last person to see him alive.'

'If you were, you could be the one person who can help us find out how he died,' remarked Patton, briskly. He turned the pages, and saw a second copy of the first page. 'Did you bring two copies of the passenger list?'

'Yes, sir.'

'You ought to join the police.' Patton gave a fleeting smile, and handed a copy to Carlsen. 'Can you have that teletyped to Captain Johnson—Caleb Johnson, at my office? ... Thanks. Now!' He ran his gaze down the list of fifty-seven passengers, ticked off those who had bought tickets in Los Angeles or anywhere near by, and asked Carlsen: 'When you're talking to Captain Johnson tell him to take a close look at those I've ticked, will you?' He nodded to the pretty girl, motioned to a chair by his side, and began to question her as she sat down.

In the next hour, he questioned all the crew, and gradually a picture emerged. It was confused and yet some kind of pattern began to form. The time was established when Miraldi had last been seen to be awake. Three hostesses had noticed him looking at the Grand Canyon; he had been an exceptionally refined-looking man and young women were likely to take especial notice of him. He had settled down as if to sleep very soon afterwards, and no one had ever seen him move again.

To everyone he questioned, Patton said: 'I need to know who passed him around the time he went to sleep.'

There had been so many. The hostesses and one steward could recall a red-haired girl, a very old man, a woman carrying a baby, another child holding her skirts, but no one else for certain.

'Keep thinking, keep remembering,' Patton urged before he let them go.

A messenger arrived from the hospital with the contents of Miraldi's pockets, but nothing seemed of interest. Then word came that the sweepings of the cabin had been emptied into a plastic bag. The bag was brought in and Carlsen, Patton and one other officer began to go through it.

They found the screwed-up sketch of the amphitheatre, the dots and the ringed dots, the cryptic notes in Miraldi's rather pale handwriting. Obviously these referred to what had happened at the amphitheatre.

There was a copy of *Student Action* with pictures of rifle-carrying, masked National Guardsmen attacking some students, mostly girls. The one-word caption was: *'Brutes'*. Miraldi had marked this with a cross; and had also marked several of the articles, drawing attention to vicious, near-seditious phrases and to calls for *Student Action*. There was no doubt: this was incitement to revolution.

There was a brief note on what had happened afterwards, at the college buildings, but Miraldi did not appear to have gone inside. He had left the campus, driven or been driven to the airport and someone had seen him and booked on the same flight; that was the only feasible explanation.

'Ah!' breathed Patton, and called Johnson. 'Caleb. Find out what time Miraldi's ticket was issued and concentrate on everyone who booked in after him. That should narrow the field.'

'Okay,' said Johnson as he rang off.

Then, for the first time since he had heard about Miraldi's death, Randy Patton relaxed. It felt as if all the blood in his body had thinned, every nerve tingled, the back of his head, his neck and his shoulders were tight and painful. But he was done, as nearly as he could be. Carlsen, proving very human, sent for coffee and sat sipping it with him, noticing how pale Patton was, and still marvelling at his tremendous concentration of energy.

Then, suddenly, Patton sat bolt upright, thrust his cup on the desk and rasped: 'What time is it?'

'Two-thirty, near enough,' Carlsen answered.

'Thank God for that,' Patton said in a cracked voice. 'My daughter's due in at two-fifty on TWA Flight 8012 from Denver, Colorado. I'd forgotten, would you believe it?'

Carlsen said helpfully: 'I'll check the flight number and time of arrival, Commissioner. You just stay there and relax.'

Relax, thought Patton, and almost groaned, as anxiety for Dodie swept over him like an avalanche.

CHAPTER FIVE

MORE TROUBLE

Dodie came out of the swinging doors, tall and fresh and attractive in a linen dress of green, short but not ridiculously so, nor over-seductive, carrying a lemon-coloured coat over her arm, a purse and a small overnight case. Her waist was so slim there seemed no possibility that she was pregnant. She looked about at once, not seeing her father, then suddenly her eyes lit up and she moved towards him, backing away to avoid crossing the path of a young soldier who was eyeing her with open admiration.

Patton thought: Well, she doesn't show.

And she looked wonderful, not even dishevelled.

'Daddy!'

'Honey!'

They hugged a moment and then drew apart. His gaze searched hers, questioningly, and he thought that she looked puzzled. He took her bag.

'Is this all you've got?'

'Yes. I have to fly back in the morning,' she added to his surprise. 'Did you drive yourself?'

'Yes,' he answered. 'My car's outside.' He had asked Carlsen to bring it along to the main exit doors and had no doubt that it would be there.

'Goodie,' she said, as she had so often as a child. 'We can talk as we drive home.'

'Home' wasn't home, really; they had no shared home. But for an hour or two it would serve well enough. He started out striding, realised he was going too fast for her, and then suddenly stopped in his tracks, as what she said dawned on him.

'You're going back in the *morning*?'

'Daddy, I must. There's a flight at half-past eleven.'

'Honey, what's so important that you had to fly three-quarters of the way across the continent for a few hours?'

'I'll tell you about it soon,' she said. 'Not here.'

His gaze dropped again to her slim waist, and he wondered if there could possibly be anything else, then rejected the thought. But she looked so good; wholesome. Worried, perhaps, but—well, good was the only word.

His car was there with Carlsen by the door.

'Lieutenant,' Patton said. 'This is my daughter Dodie.' He allowed barely time for smiles and nods before going on: 'You'll ask my office not to disturb me at my apartment unless it's urgent, won't you?'

Carlsen, who always wanted to be a step ahead, said: 'I've fixed that, sir.'

'Good. Thanks. Good night.'

Soon they were settled in the car, Dodie by Patton's side, bag and coat in the back. He knew the road as well as he knew Fifth Avenue, and soon they were on the Expressway heading for Queensborough Bridge. There was comparatively little traffic, most of what there was going too fast. Why weren't some of them being stopped? A siren wailed and he relaxed.

'All right,' he said. 'When is it to be?'

He knew she was staring at him, puzzled.

'When's what to be?' she asked.

'Let me put it another way,' he said, determined to maintain a light hearted note; the very last thing he must do was show the slightest sign of being the heavy father. 'Who's the lucky man?'

There was no response, and Dodie continued to stare at him. He snatched a glance at her, taking his eyes off the road for a split second. She looked so beautiful in the half-light from the tall lamps and the passing headlights; her eyes really did look like stars. He turned back to the road, as a Jaguar growled past them. What was the matter? Was she so nervous of him that she didn't want to think he had guessed?

She gave a little gasp of sound; then a tiny stifled laugh. Her hand rested on his arm for a moment, feather-light.

'Oh, Daddy,' she said. 'How old-fashioned can you get?'

'Old-fashioned?' he echoed, piqued.

'Yes, Daddy dear,' she went on, a chuckle making her voice ripple. 'If I ever became pregnant by accident, I would *not* alarm you like this. I—well, I'm not going to take the risk, anyhow,' she added, and lightly. 'Didn't you know my heart was still in England, with Gordon Scott?'

'He's a long way off,' Patton pointed out gruffly. 'Young people have to live.'

'I think we're going to have to talk about this another time,' said Dodie, primly. 'You've obviously got a lot to learn about our generation. This particular member of it anyhow.' She squeezed his arm, and he stifled the impulse to ask: 'If I'm wrong, what *is* the trouble?'

Could it be money?

At least he wouldn't put words into her mouth again.

'Daddy,' she said at last. 'Do you remember at Christmas we were talking about campus rebels and suchlike?'

He was so astonished that he switched his gaze to her again; but this time she was staring straight ahead and didn't notice the effect on him.

'Yes,' he answered. 'I asked you to let me know if anything seemed to be brewing at Boulder.'

He remembered thinking at the time that it was like turning his daughter into a spy; and he remembered laughing the thought off.

'That's right,' she said.

'Is something brewing?' Patton demanded, his heart sinking.

She turned to look at him and said quite positively: 'I'm afraid it is. I've been wondering whether I ought to write to you about it. I nearly did, last week, but I was so busy. Then today, there was the trouble at Mid-Cal, and—Daddy, I'm scared.'

'Scared?'

'Yes. I think they are going to stir up trouble at Boulder, too.'

'In the same way as it was stirred at Mid-Cal?'

'Yes.' She spoke as if she had no doubt at all, and it went through him like a knife-thrust. Yet she was on edge, too, much more sensitive about this than about his suspicions that she was pregnant. 'Daddy, don't laugh at me, will you?'

'No,' said Patton, taking a hand off the wheel and pressing her knee. 'No, I won't laugh, Dodie. What's scaring you?' All he could see except for the road was the campus at Mid-Cal. The fighting, the tear gas, the bottle and rock throwing.

'There are several students at Boulder who seem set on stirring up grievances. I simply didn't dare to telephone you in case I was overheard. Two or three groups have been forming

40

to resist any trouble. They've met in secret, making plans to counter the troublemakers. Several members of these peace-promoting groups have been beaten up.'

Patton felt cold as ice.

'Badly hurt?' he asked, sharply.

'No. Just warned off.'

'You mean before the actual trouble starts the organisers want to cow the students and discourage opposition?' Patton asked as if it hurt him to speak.

'Yes, that's exactly it,' Dodie stated flatly. 'Most of the students will listen. They don't mean any harm but they get a kick out of demonstrations. They'll go whichever way they're pushed. But Boulder's run so well, there aren't really any grounds for complaint, so when these new students started stirring up trouble, they—well, I've told you. We decided to combat it early. Only someone either heard what we were planning, or was one of us, and told the troublemakers. There's a tense atmosphere on the campus, Daddy. A lot of students are scared and at least as many angry. I . . .' She broke off, gripped his arm again and went on in a husky voice: 'I was afraid that if I spent a long time on the telephone about it, someone would find out. That's why I had to come and see you. I was right to come, wasn't I?'

Very slowly and deliberately, Randy Patton answered:

'You couldn't have been more right.' He turned off towards the bridge and soon they were on the high level, seeing the myriad lamps of Queen's and the other bridges, the lights in the great tall buildings in a skyline which seemed as if it had been cut out of the dark sky by giant scissors. 'Let's be quiet a minute, honey.' He needed time to absorb all she had told him, to see it in its right perspective. He had been worried from the start, appalled by Miraldi's death, but in a way this made him feel worse than anything that had gone before. The fact that a few newly enrolled students at such a university as Boulder could spread deep alarm among the ordinary students was appalling.

At last, he broke his silence.

'How many troublemakers are there?'

Dodie had obviously expected the question.

'About ten or twelve.'

'Can you name them?'

'Oh, yes.' She was positive.

'How many of your friends are nervous of them?'

'A lot are angry, but...' Dodie broke off, as if she hardly knew what to say, but soon she cleared away that apprehension. 'Daddy, we don't *want* trouble. We don't want anything to interrupt the last month of the semester. We—oh, we're scared, I suppose.'

'Have you made any specific complaints?' asked Patton.

'To the faculty, you mean?'

'Yes.'

'No,' she answered. 'I doubt if they realise what's going on. Oh, some of them may, but there's no sign that they think it's serious. But I'm scared, I really am.'

'Of what might happen to you?'

'No, silly!' She was dangerously near exasperation point. 'Everything's so good at Boulder. It's been a happy place ever since I've been going there and I hate to think of anything happening as it's happening at Mid-Cal. *Is* that as bad as it seemed to be on television?' she asked.

'Yes,' answered Patton simply. He was silent again for a few minutes before asking: 'Can you really name these trouble-makers?'

'Nine of them, anyhow,' she assured him. 'And they're all on the staff of the campus rag—*Student Action*.' She took a folded newspaper from her handbag, smoothed it out and held it towards him.

The picture of masked, rifle-carrying National Guardsmen and the girl students was there, with the caption 'Brutes'. Some other pages were different, including a centre page on which was a group of students. She had marked nine of them with an X, much as Miraldi had.

'Those I've marked always stir up trouble,' she stated simply.

'Can it be proved they've been involved in seditious and revolutionary talk?'

'I suppose it could,' said Dodie with obvious reluctance, 'but that might create the very atmosphere they want. Daddy...'

'Yes?'

'I was hoping ...' Dodie hesitated, staring at the narrow chasm of the street as they moved along it. 'I was hoping perhaps you could tip off the Boulder police and just have these students held. I mean, I suppose it's impossible, but if they could be taken away quietly and without any warning, it would make such a difference. If there's any warning then— well, even a lot of old students who would take no part in demonstrations would swing over to them. Until now I'd no idea what stubborn creatures people *are*.'

'Plain 'ornery,' agreed Patton, forcing a note of laughter into his voice. 'We can't just go in by dead of night, like secret police, and haul them away. Then the fat would be in the fire. But we can do something, honey.' He turned up Sixth Avenue, almost deserted and with few lights on in the high buildings. He could not make up his mind how much to tell her about Mid-Cal, and Miraldi; and by the time they reached his apartment he had decided to say very little. If the Press once learned what the police suspected about Miraldi then it would be front-page news all over the country, possibly all over the world.

He parked the car and then walked Dodie to the main doors of the apartment building. Suddenly, his fingers tightened on her arm, for he saw a shadowy figure move inside the foyer, and there was no night porter there. It could be a man from Headquarters with information for him, or . . .

A man stepped forward, obviously not trying to conceal his presence. At first, Patton didn't recognise him; in fact, Dodie did, first. She gave a little choking cry and rushed forward. To his astonishment she leapt into the man's arms which fastened about her, hugging her with almost savage power. They kissed, completely oblivious of him.

'Good grief!' exclaimed Patton, as he realised that this was Gordon Scott, from Dawlish's department in London. Surprise melted in a different emotion, amazement at the passion evident in both of them. How desperately Dodie was in love with this man! He went ahead and pressed for the elevator, and when the doors opened, he coughed and asked: 'Anyone coming in?'

Only then did they separate; but they clutched hands in the elevator, at the landing, in the apartment, as first Scott and then Dodie talked. Gradually, the picture formed in Patton's mind. As soon as it had become clear that the trouble at Mid-Cal was on a big scale, Dawlish had sent Scott over so that he could assess the situation on the spot, and also tell Patton things which Dawlish hadn't felt wise to discuss over the telephone.

At Avon University in Warwickshire there were rumours of major trouble. And this was true also of Border University, just over the border in Scotland. Meanwhile, warnings of impending trouble were coming from all the cities Dawlish had mentioned on the telephone, and several others.

'What the Deputy Commissioner would like, sir,' said Gordon Scott, a fair haired, fresh-faced, firm-chinned youngster with blue-grey eyes which sparkled despite his travel tiredness, 'is to find out if there is any overall pattern in the disturbances or the threatened disturbances over here, linking them to those in other countries. And he would like specimens of the publication *Student Action* from every campus.'

'Is it so widespread?' Dodie asked. They were in the kitchen, her father sprawling back in an easy chair, drinking coffee, Dodie at the sink rinsing cups, Scott sitting on the working top close to her.

'Let's put it this way,' said Scott. 'It's in so many places that we know that the great Patrick D. thinks it may be in a lot of others we don't yet even suspect. Hence the inquiries and the coming special session. Have you any preference where that session should be, sir?' he asked Patton.

'Not in the U.S.A.,' Patton repeated. 'I still don't care where I have to go.' He was caught out by a gargantuan yawn, and jumped to his feet. 'I'm going to get some sleep,' he said. 'You two should do the same. Good to see you, Gordon.' He went over and kissed Dodie on the cheek. 'I now see how wrong I was,' he added, with a grin.

'You should be ashamed,' reproved Dodie.

'What's all this about?' asked Gordon Scott.

'It's a family secret,' Dodie retorted.

'How soon can I join the family?' asked Scott.

All three of them stood absolutely still. A little colour tinged Dodie's cheeks and her eyes had never seemed so bright. Scott seemed to pale. Then he coughed, put his arm round Dodie's shoulders, and went on in a husky voice:

'I didn't mean to blurt it out like that, but having said it, I mean it absolutely. Dodie knows I'm in love with her. I would never have believed I could feel as I do. It—I mean she— obsesses me, sir. What I want to do above everything else in the world is to marry Dodie. I would do anything, even resign from the Metropolitan Police, if I had to.' The pressure of his arm was obviously increasing all the time, and his fingers were

44

biting into the top of Dodie's shoulder. With tremendous intensity, he went on: 'Do you have any objection, sir?'

Patton looked at him, searchingly; as searchingly at Dodie. He could see her heart in her eyes. He was deeply touched because he knew that his approval would mean so much to her; touched, also, because it also mattered to Gordon Scott.

'No,' he said at last. 'I've no objection. But I hope you'll both think of all the angles before you decide when to marry and where to live.' Suddenly, totally unexpectedly, his voice broke. 'Just keep a spare bed for me,' he said, and swung round and strode to his room. 'I'm overtired,' he muttered to himself, almost angrily. 'Tired out, in fact.' He took off his clothes and got into bed in the buff, lacking the energy to put on pyjamas or to wash. Lying wide awake and staring at the ceiling and the red flicker of a neon sign from a delicatessen reflected on the windows, he wondered: Did Pat Dawlish send Scott over because he knew how he felt? The son-of-a-gun, I bet he did!

Soon afterwards, Patton fell asleep. He was quite oblivious when Dodie came in, and stood looking down at him as the red light flickered on his face.

She turned back to Gordon Scott, who was just behind her.

'I wish he could find someone to be happy with,' she said. 'He's so lonely. So very lonely.'

'The great Pat Dawlish says he's the most dedicated policeman he's ever met in his life,' Scott said. 'His work must be a help.'

He had a strange feeling that he had said the wrong thing.

CHAPTER SIX

THE GREAT PAT DAWLISH

Dawlish sat in his office at the top of the old building of New Scotland Yard, studying the written reports which were already coming in from university cities all over the world. It was middle afternoon on the third day after he had talked to Patton in New York, and a great deal had happened since then. Just how much, he couldn't yet assess.

Along two walls in this large room was a long, sloping bench, rather like a row of old-fashioned office desks of the kind at which one stood or else sat on high stools. But there was, in fact, nothing remotely old-fashioned about either the room or the bench. The room had been completely modernised when Dawlish had taken over, and the furniture, if stark, had both simplicity and comfort. Even the windows had been widened, to give more light and a better view. On one side were relief maps of the world, beautifully executed; on the other, a plain map of the Mercator Projection, showing every major city and location of every major police office. Similar maps were already installed in the police headquarters of many major cities, and an electronic system was built in, by which messages could be sent out to each of these cities. Dawlish had only to press a tiny button, little larger than a pin-head, to be in radio-telephone touch with any other similar office, and, to reduce the risk of being coherently overheard, the voices at either end of the message were 'scrambled'. Whenever a message came in a red light showed at the pinheads.

None glowed at this moment.

Dawlish put down a report, written in formal but excellent English, from Tokyo. The Director General of the National Police Agency was obviously perturbed by the situation: and in a city where university disturbances had often reached the proportions of serious riots, his anxiety was understandable. Beneath it was a shorter report from Bonn. The West German

Chief of Police said briskly: 'It is not expected that the trouble will get out of hand, but our experience and advice is at the service of the conference. We suggest the special session be at Frankfurt or Brussels.'

Dawlish found himself smiling faintly.

The International Police Conference, known more colloquially as the Crime Haters, had grown up haphazardly, and the West German Police had never really approved of this. The conference had first been convened over ten years earlier, at a time when it was realised by most national authorities that crime and criminals were no longer halted by frontiers. Major crimes of forgery, bullion robbery, art thefts, drug-running, arms-running, were committed almost with impunity at the time when there had been little or no consultation between police forces, not even those virtually next door to one another. Police forces of nations, like the judiciary, were often very different, even though the methods of detection were similar the world over. A number of major crimes had led to conferences of a few nations which had gradually been increased until, at this time, the police forces of over a hundred nations were members of the conference.

For years the sessions had been held first in one country and then another; the delegate in the host city had been both convenor and chairman, and on the host police force had fallen the responsibility of organising the session, arranging hotels, assembly and lecture rooms. The big forces found this practicable, small ones found it too burdensome. The time was obviously not far off when there would have to be a world secretariat and some permanent headquarters where an emergency session could be held at short notice. Here in London, in fact in all the major cities in the west, the tourist season was at its height and it simply wouldn't be possible to accommodate hundreds of delegates; and there would be at least two from each member nation.

That was a major problem.

Another, greater one, was to cope with the actual system of receiving, sifting and acting on reports. It wasn't Dawlish's responsibility, but he was doing a great deal to relieve it. So also was Van Woelden in Amsterdam, and several others. Randy Patton had more than enough to do in the United States, although only yesterday he had arranged to work with the Canadian and the West Indian authorities.

47

Trouble threatened, everywhere.

It would be bad enough if they were fully equipped to cope, thought Dawlish. But they weren't. Given another year the secretariat would—or should—be in being, but even then the problems would be formidable. Some of the nations called on to contribute to the total cost had made difficulties; and there was a certain amount of stiff competition for the honour of being the host city.

Whatever these problems, the urgent one now concerned the student revolts.

Dawlish had marked in ink a phrase or two from many reports.

'The situation in Paris/Sorbonne is extremely grave,' the Paris report stated. 'Serious outbreaks are clearly close to the surface. If police and/or military action is taken too soon, however, it could worsen and not improve the situation.'

'Here the problem at the Eire New University is precarious,' said the report from Dublin.

'We have reason to fear that a student revolt larger than any we have experienced before may develop before the end of the year.'

That came from Sweden.

'Large-scale precautions including the deployment of troops to reinforce the police have been taken, and the authorisation given for the use of riot sticks, smoke bombs and, as a last resort, small arms fire,' reported Tokyo.

'In spite of a long course of propaganda on the importance of peaceful means of progress there are indications that some violence might occur.'

That was New Delhi, about a university opened only a year earlier, near Benares.

Dawlish put these aside, and stood up. He was a massive man, six feet three inches tall and broad in proportion. His beautifully tailored suit emphasised not only his size but his physical fitness. His corn-coloured hair crimped slightly, his face was tanned more golden than brown. But for a broken nose, souvenir of schoolday boxing, he would have been remarkably handsome. As it was, he was extremely impressive, the more so when he frowned. With so much on his mind, so much anxiety and so much to do, having to worry about the venue of the session was infuriating. Yet he had put out feelers in London and Paris, as well as New York. The accommodation simply didn't exist. And there was no time, even if it were desirable, to try to arrange for the London police to take delegates into their homes.

He looked out over London; the great loops in the Thames, the London County Hall and the Festival Hall across the river, Westminster Bridge below him, St. Paul's part of the skyline broken now by some square, squat, modern buildings. There was not an inspiration in sight. He went back to his desk, then pressed for Van Woelden in Amsterdam; at once an assistant, followed immediately afterwards by the Dutch Chief of Police himself, was on the line.

'Have you some brainwave, Pat?' Van Woelden asked.

'I'm not even sure I've got a brain,' Dawlish replied. 'Will it help if we go through the applications for conferences one by one?'

'New and old,' mused Van Woelden.

'Yes. We may have overlooked something.'

'I have my copy of the file in front of me, Patrick.'

Dawlish stretched out for his, and began to glance through it.

'So have I ... Addis Ababa ... Stop if we come to a possible ... Aden ... Andorra ...' He reached the F's, and the Dutchman had not interrupted. 'Golana,' he went on, turning over a brochure. 'I ...' He stopped, frowning, and repeated: 'Golana.'

'Are you serious?' asked Van Woelden.

'A new, central African state,' Dawlish commented, looking at the picture of the youthful prime minister of Golana. 'We've never held one in Africa ... And if you look at the brochure ...' He paused, only to go on: 'A new airfield with four runways each large enough for any jet aircraft except the monsters. A new university almost finished, small by American and European standards but by emergent countries' standards, quite large. There is room for a thousand students and faculty buildings for one hundred professors and staff, built on the motel principle and surrounding the main university building.' He broke off as his voice began to rise.

'Patrick!' The Dutchman sounded excited, too. 'It is to be opened in September this year. In three months. There are all facilities ... it would kill two birds with one stone. Will you talk to the Golanan ambassador in London?'

'Yes,' Dawlish said, briskly. 'As soon as I've some news, I'll call you back.' He put down the receiver but before moving again, looked more closely at the brochure. The land about Gola, the capital of Golana, was hilly and pleasant-looking, the buildings had the modern touch but there was palm-tree landscaping at least in the pictures. He saw a phrase: 'Equidistant between the major international airfields of Nairobi and Johannesburg'. He pushed the brochure aside, and then lifted another telephone. At the same time he pressed a button on his desk and asked for the private number of a Permanent Secretary at the Foreign Office who regarded himself as a Very Important Person.

The door from the next room opened and a middle-aged man appeared, Chief Inspector Sills, who was standing in for Gordon Scott. Childs, Dawlish's assistant for many years, had only recently retired. Sills was only learning the job, but he had one extremely good qualification: he could speak several foreign languages fluently. For a long time he had been a travelling adviser attached to New Scotland Yard and had visited the police headquarters in many parts of the world.

'Sills, how well do you know Golana? ... *Lord Seveston, please ... Yes, I'll hold on ... The Deputy Assistant Commissioner at Scotland Yard.*' As he spoke he looked his question to Sills.

'Reasonably well, sir.'

'How well?'

'When I was there, they had a very good second-in-command of the police, sir—M'gobo, Sebastian M'gobo. I believe he's now the chief of police since they retired all European officers.'

'Very good, did you say?'

'Yes, sir. I liked both Golana and M'gobo.'

'*Yes. I'll hold on.*' Dawlish didn't look away from Sills. 'Why did you like the country?'

'Pleasant climate, sir—nowhere on the plateau is below four thousand feet so it's seldom too hot or too cold. Very pleasant people, too. They—er—they kicked us out, sir, but they did it barefoot and with a smile, if you know what I mean.'

'I do. We're thinking of it for an emergency session ... Hallo, Tubby! ... How are you? ... Wonderful!' He actually infused enthusiasm into his voice. 'My dear chap, I'd love to. Meanwhile ... In my official capacity, of course ... Do you know the Golanan ambassador well? ... Good! ... Is he very

50

stuffy and formal or could I break diplomatic barriers? ...
Well, you know this circus I've become involved with ...' He
looked up to see Sills smothering a grin. 'Good Lord! You
actually know the name? ... Well, we need to hold a special
session lasting four or five days at the most, and we wondered ...'

He paused, to listen, and slowly a smile spread over his face
and he cocked a thumb at Sills.

'Will you?' he said at last. 'Wonderful! I'd be available any
time within the next two hours. I can't thank you enough,
Tubby. I really can't.' He put down the receiver, leaned back
in his chair and said to Sills: 'The Permanent Secretary at
the Foreign Office says he thinks they will jump at this chance.
They feel isolated out there and this could get them off to a
good start with the university becoming a convention centre
during vacation periods. Damned funny how things work out
sometimes, isn't it? ... Obviously our chaps could fly commercial flights to Nairobi and Johannesburg, and perhaps
Salisbury and Bulawayo ... Tell you what, Sills. Check the
flights from the major cities, all the cities, in the conference.
Then tackle BOAC, Air France, KLM, Qantas, every company which has flights direct to Nairobi or you know where,
and find out whether they would make a stop at Gola.'

'Right, sir!' Sills turned quickly.

'Get two or three other chaps on it, too. Oh, don't forget
TWA and Pan Am.'

Sills disappeared with another: 'Right, sir.'

Dawlish sat back.

Throughout his life he had acted on what others called
hunches and which to him were a form of intelligent deduction
allied to a feeling in his bones that what he was about to do
was the right thing. Now, for the first time since he had been
alerted to the student troubles, he leaned back at full length
and relaxed. He actually closed his eyes.

It was a good time for him, personally, to be away. His wife
Felicity, bless her, was relative-visiting in Scotland and Ire-
land and would be away for at least another week.

It was time they had a holiday together.

Soon, he made himself sit bolt upright, and pulled the
American file to him. Here were reports and recordings of
messages from Randy Patton and from Gordon Scott: most
he had read several times, some he hadn't yet read thoroughly.

51

They were very precise; indeed, Patton's was almost laconic.

'Miraldi died from aconite poisoning, supposedly put into his drink as he turned to watch the Grand Canyon. Death was virtually instantaneous. Notes and sketches by him show indication that in the amphitheatre where the trouble started one spy, or troublemaker, had been posted to every hundred or so students. We strongly suspect Miraldi was followed from Mid-Cal to Airport L.A. Three passengers booked tickets after he booked his: Mepita Gonzales, Mexican-speaking wife of farm-worker, not suspected. Jonathan Tyson, aged twenty-two, address in Santa Margarita, student U.C.L.A., suspected. William S. Kelly, aged twenty-one, motor-mechanic from San Francisco, suspected. Photographs of both to follow.'

There was a further note:

'The first victim of the trouble, Gerald Lee, appears to have attempted to avoid the amphitheatre, nevertheless he was attacked and died in hospital. His sister Catherine and three girl students, triplets, Mary, Marie and Maria Pentecost, were witnesses. Descriptions of two assailants approximate W. S. Kelly and Jonathan Tyson.'

And a third note said:

'Students still in control at Mid-Cal. State Governor considering (i) deployment strong force armed police and national guard, (ii) asking Washington for troops.'

And a fourth:

'Similar outbreak planned Boulder U. Colo. Disruptive elements identified and four students found to have incendiary bombs in their possession. All four arrested and charged.'

Dawlish thought: Mary, Marie and Maria Pentecost. And he thought: Poor devil, kicked to death. Earlier reports told him how badly Dodie Patton had been scared; and other students at Boulder. Here was a youth who had defied the rabble-rousers callously kicked to death.

He gave a little shiver and the telephone bell rang. He snatched the instrument up.

'Deputy A.C.,' he answered, as laconically as Patton had written.

'His Excellency the Ambassador of the State of Golana wishes to speak to you,' a man stated with great precision. 'Will you be good enough to hold on?'

Golana was one of the small mid-African states which had become independent only three years before. It was surrounded by other newly independent nations, with the Congo on the north-west and Kenya on the north-east, Tanzania along its eastern frontier and Zambia to the south. It was virtually an island, with the vast lake Tia-Tia its southern boundary and great rivers forming the other boundaries, the largest was the River Gola. These natural boundaries had really decided its size, and although English, Belgian and German influences were very strong, the firmly coalescing factor was tribal: only three tribes had ever inhabited the land of the rivers.

By far the largest, the Golas, closely related to the Basutos further south, had a long history of peace, and many tribal leaders had been among the first to send members of the tribes to be educated in Europe. They had, therefore, been much more prepared than most to take over their country. Left to themselves they would have had little trouble, despite the problems of a landlocked nation whose goods could only be sent to Europe and America by agreement with its neighbours. The nations on every side, however, had acute and urgent political problems; and Golana had great difficulty in staying neutral.

Nevertheless, she had succeeded so far.

Now, to establish not only her independence but her economy, she needed many friends outside Africa.

CHAPTER SEVEN

VENUE

'Mr. Deputy Assistant Commissioner?'

'Your Excellency,' Dawlish said.

'I understand from Lord Seveston of the Foreign Office that you have some interest in holding a conference in Golana.' The ambassador's voice was very deep, very resonant.

'I have, indeed, sir.'

'May I ask when such a conference would begin and how long it would continue?'

'By next weekend, if at all possible. And for four or five days, although if it were practical I have no doubt that some delegates would like to stay longer.'

'And are the delegates members of the police force?'

'Delegates would come from over a hundred police forces throughout the world,' Dawlish explained. 'I would expect about two hundred and fifty.'

'Mr. Deputy,' said the ambassador, 'will you be good enough to inform me of the nature of this conference and why it has to be held at such short notice?'

'The official study is of drugs, the real subject is student unrest at universities,' answered Dawlish. 'And there is new urgency in view of riots in the past few days.'

'I *see*,' responded the ambassador, as if indeed the answer was a revelation. 'It will be necessary for me to make representations to my government, you understand. If the reply is favourable, may I assume that you have authority to proceed?'

'I would have to consult colleagues,' Dawlish said, and for the first time there was a slight hesitation at the other end. Thoughtfully, he went on: 'Would it be wise for me to get the agreement of my colleagues in advance?'

'Yes,' answered the ambassador, and hesitated before asking: 'Will it take long?'

'No more than an hour,' Dawlish assured him.

'Then within two hours after your confirmation I will have the answer,' promised the ambassador. 'Will you be good enough to call me and state your name—then there will be no delay.'

'You're very good,' said Dawlish. 'I will.'

He pressed for Sills as he replaced the receiver, and before the man was right inside the room, he said: 'Get me Woelden, Lutsi of Tokyo, Neilsen of Stockholm, Targett of Canberra and Patton—oh: and y Fernandes of the Argentine. Hold them on—I won't be more than a minute or two with each.' As Sills turned, he called: 'If they all accept Golana as the venue, we'll go ahead.'

Sills turned again.

'Then shouldn't we check with Moscow and New Delhi, sir?'

Dawlish grinned. 'What's happening to me? Yes, of course.'

In two minutes he was talking to Van Woelden, who said: 'I am in complete agreement.' Neilsen answered briskly: 'Anywhere, provided it is soon. Mr. Dawlish, we had some shooting at Uppsala.' He spoke as if that were utterly unbelievable. As he finished Solatov, the Chief of Police in Moscow, came on the line. 'Such a venue appears to me wholly satisfactory, Mr. Deputy.' 'It is with great pleasure that I agree,' said Lutsi. 'I ask, please, for the utmost expedition. Already at Kyoto, in the past peaceful, there has been a demonstration.' Next, Targett said: 'It's all right with me, Dawlish. How soon? ... Next Wednesday, I can make it.' Carlos y Fernandez, of the Argentine, demurred: 'It will perhaps be inconvenient, Mr. Dawlish, but in a matter of such urgency I would not oppose.'

Finally, there was Patton.

'Randy,' said Dawlish. 'Would Golana be agreeable to you? They have all the facilities in the new Gola University which won't open until September.'

'Certainly,' Patton replied. 'Anywhere would be right if it can be quick.'

'Next Wednesday or Thursday,' said Dawlish.

'It's good to know you can still move quickly,' Patton said drily. 'We've had four more trouble spots—in Oregon, Minnesota, Mississippi and New Mexico. In three the students have been armed. No major clash so far, but ...'

'Randy,' Dawlish interrupted, 'how about the suspects, Kelly and Tyson?'

'We haven't picked them up yet,' answered Patton. 'We're getting identikit likenesses prepared. The minute there's any news, you shall have it.'

'Thanks,' Dawlish said warmly.

He rang off, leaned back and ran his massive hand across his forehead. It was wet. He often forgot how much tension there was in such a situation and how much energy he used while sitting at his desk. He did not even begin to suspect the way the police chiefs respected and admired him. He had a rare quality of allying speed with effectiveness.

Sills came in, and frowned.

'Are you all right, sir?'

'I'm a bit hot,' Dawlish admitted.

'You can overdo it, sir.'

'And I probably shall. Stand by for a teletype to go out to all the delegate countries, will you?'

'All I need is the message, sir.'

Dawlish had a hand on the telephone. .

'How about the airline companies?'

'BOAC. Qantas, KLM and South African Airways will all play, sir. I've got BOAC preparing a complete list of scheduled flights.'

Dawlish was dialling.

'Don't let me keep you,' he said, and a moment later was answered by a girl with a pleasant voice, obviously not native English. 'The ambassador is expecting a call from me; my name is Dawlish, Deputy Assistant Commissioner Dawlish.'

'Just one moment, please.'

The ambassador was on the line so quickly that it was almost as if he had been waiting anxiously for this call.

'You have been very quick, Mr. Deputy.' He listened intently, before saying: 'I am *very* gratified, and I shall telephone Gola at once. Will you be in your office for the next hour?'

'Until I hear from you,' Dawlish said. 'Do you expect any difficulties, Mr. Ambassador?'

'I do not expect any but I am always prepared for some,' said the ambassador urbanely. 'Goodbye.'

Dawlish smiled a little ruefully as he rang off, considered for a few moments, and then called Sills. Sills must think that he was running on some kind of electronic power; strange how the man made him, Dawlish, feel that he just couldn't stop.

'I think we're all right,' he said. 'Be all ready for the word "go".' Then he pulled the American reports towards him, and thought of Patton and the identikit pictures of the two suspects of Miraldi's murder. Scanning the report he came across the names of the triplets: Marie, Mary and Maria Pentecost. Who would name her daughters to allow of such confusion? He stifled a laugh, then read again their story of what had happened at Santa Margarita.

Marie, Mary and Maria lived in the shadow of police protection.

They had not been back to the campus since the night of the outbreak; at least half of the students were from California or neighbouring states, and either stayed home or with close friends. Up at the University College itself the police and National Guard still surrounded the main building. Professor Connell, Philip Pardoe and Professor Armour were still hostages, as well as three other professors held in a different room. So far as one could judge, none was hurt.

Kalta spoke over the main microphone every hour during the day, and his threat was always the same.

'If the police try to get in, we'll cut six professorial throats.' No one doubted that he meant it.

There was something remote and almost unreal about the present situation, about being accompanied everywhere by the police. And no matter how they or anyone else tried, they always came back to the same, haunting subject.

'If only we'd gone back sooner,' Mary said. She was slightly smaller and perhaps the most attractive of the sisters. 'He wouldn't have been attacked. He would be alive today.'

'Mary, honey,' Marie told her gently, 'it won't help to blame yourself.' Often mistaken in looks for Maria, her voice was softer, holding a pleasing singing lilt. She parted her hair on the left side, while Maria parted hers on the right; it was said that without this help, even their parents would not be able to tell them apart. 'Gerald wouldn't blame you.'

'Well, *I* blame myself,' Mary said bitterly.

'Honey, you're flagellating yourself, and you don't need to.' Maria was brisk-voiced and quite sharp in manner, a more positive person than either of her sisters. 'You *really* don't need to. And it's immaterial whether Gerald would have blamed you. Cathy doesn't and her folk don't, either. You won't help them or anyone else by blaming yourself.'

There were tears in Mary's eyes as she listened.

They were in the grounds of their home overlooking Santa Margarita Bay, just now ablaze with sun. A few tall pines bent towards the land, fringing the bay, while more trees rose from the sand dunes beyond. Here and there houses—some very like their own—were visible among the foliage. It was quite beautiful, a perfect setting for the girls. They were in bikinis, sunbathing by the pool which was built in sand dunes, all three tanned the same golden brown hue. Twenty yards or so to the left was a police officer; on the other side were two more, one of whom was leaning against a tree and watching the girls with admiration; the other's glances were keener, but less open.

They heard a car approach the house. At one time they would not have noticed it, but now they were ultra-sensitive. The turn of their heads, the twist of their tanned bodies, showed their uneasiness. Soon, the door on to the patio of the house opened and Mrs. Pentecost appeared, grey-haired but almost as slim and quite as attractive as her daughters.

'You've a police visitor,' she called.

In fact, two men appeared behind her, one grey and elderly, the other just over medium height, fair-haired and, in a rugged way, handsome. At sight of him all three girls seemed to go still, as if paralysed. Their mother was as surprised as the two men. The guarding police drew nearer, suddenly alert and wary.

'Oh *no*,' Mary almost groaned. 'Oh dear God!'

Maria put a hand on her arm, protectively. All three stared, as if at a ghost. The grey-haired police officer looked curiously at the man whom he had brought with him.

'What's going on?' he asked, forcing himself to sound hearty. 'Haven't you seen an Englishman before? This is Mr. Scott, Gordon Scott, from Scotland Yard, London, England.'

None of the three moved towards him but Mary began to cry.

'What is this?' wondered Gordon Scott. 'What's happened to them?'

He had driven here from the airport after a flight from Los Angeles, where he had arrived the previous evening. If he had ever doubted the gravity of the situation in Santa Margarita, the newspapers and television he had seen had driven all doubts away. The student revolt here, together with the gathering threats of them elsewhere in the States, were like war-clouds. Everyone seemed to talk about them. Headlines screamed such demands as:

JAIL ALL THE BUMS
BRING UP TANKS
CIVIL RIGHTS—OR CIVIL WAR?

Demands for massive military intervention were everywhere. A few wilder newspapers even advocated dropping armed troopers. He had known how seriously Dawlish took the situation: now he knew why.

Yet the drive from the little airfield between the university campus and the town and the coast had been uneventful and pleasant, along a two-way road winding between brownish-yellow hills covered by grass which looked like corn stubble, and clumps of olive trees and juniper. Nearer the outskirts of the city there had been grass stretches outside luxurious-looking homes, more sprinklers cascading their water than he had ever seen in his life before. Six had been going round and round on the lawn outside this long, low-ceilinged house which had proved much larger inside than it had appeared.

Through the windows of an elegantly furnished room he had seen the garden, the pool and the three girls; all quite lovely. It was almost as if they were painted against the blue of the sea and the dark green of the pine trees. As impressionable as any young man, he had watched with kindling eye, until quite suddenly the girls had behaved as if terrified of him.

And the one in the middle, shorter, perhaps a little more rounded and fuller-bosomed, began to cry.

Lieutenant Spiro, who had flown up with him from Los Angeles, was a wheezy-breathing, constantly sniffing man, with a small red nose. Scott had disliked him on sight but come to appreciate a dry wit and a neat turn of phrase. There was something unconsciously funny in the way he paused after each word as he said:

'This is Mr. Scott. Gordon Scott. From Scotland Yard—London—England.' Now he looked almost suspiciously at Scott. So did the men who appeared from the sides of the garden: it was as if they expected him suddenly to attack.

Mrs. Pentecost hurried forward.

'Mary, honey, what's the matter with you?' As she passed Scott she said in an aside: 'She's been upset ever since Gerald Lee died. She thinks it's her fault. Mary, honey...'

Maria said: 'It's all right, Mother.'

'He looks so like him,' said Marie.

'So like—*whom*?' asked Mrs. Pentecost.

'Like Gerald,' answered Maria. 'He's much taller, of course, but the likeness is uncanny.'

'It's not so remarkable now,' said Maria.

Gordon Scott began to understand what had happened; and suddenly Spiro took a photograph from his pocket and looked down at it, then gave it to Scott. It was one he had seen before, of the man who had been kicked to death. There *was* a likeness about the forehead and eyes, and they were both fair: but no one who was not emotionally disturbed could have been so affected. More at ease now that he understood, he watched the little tableau break up as Mrs. Pentecost drew Mary to her.

Then Marie and Maria came forward.

'I'm sorry,' Marie said, in her softest voice, and she held out her left hand.

'I am, too,' Maria said briskly.

They shook hands, then stood on either side of Gordon Scott as Maria said with almost vexed sharpness:

'It's okay, Mary. He's not a ghost.'

'Mr. Scott,' said Maria. 'What's brought you all the way from England?'

'We're having our student troubles there and I've come to find out whether the pattern of revolt is the same here as it is there and in other countries,' Gordon replied. 'I needed to talk to someone at Santa Margarita, and Lieutenant Spiro had to come and see you, so I came along.' He was as brisk as Maria, yet as he looked at Mary his gaze and his voice were as gentle as Marie's. 'I'm sorry I startled you, Miss Pentecost. What I want to do most is to help find the murderers.'

'Of whom there were four,' stated Spiro, in his cracked voice. 'And of whom these may be two. And if they are they're wanted for two murders.'

As if by sleight of hand, he drew out two more pictures. These were not photographs but photostat copies of two made-up pictures of the suspect passengers on TWA Flight 1071 from Los Angeles to New York.

He held these towards the girls.

'How about it, ladies?' he asked.

Then he went still and silent; and so did everyone, including Mrs. Pentecost who had her arm round Mary's shoulders, and Gordon Scott himself. It was as if everyone knew how crucial the answer would be.

CHAPTER EIGHT

THE IDENTIFICATION

Maria looked very intently at the photograph, and said: 'They are two of the men who attacked Gerald.'

Maria stated: 'Yes. They're the men.'

Mary used her mother's handkerchief to dry her eyes, and said huskily: 'I shall never forget them. Never.'

Gordon Scott felt a great surge of relief; and of hope. There couldn't be the slightest doubt: these two men had first taken part in the murder of Gerald Lee, then watched and followed Miraldi. Add these two facts together and they would have enough evidence to convict. He had a sense of the tremendous significance of the identification, a sense that at last the police here had broken through. He felt almost jubilant, and yet the sorrow on the face of the girl Mary and the distress of the others touched him with something akin to embarrassment. So, he averted his gaze.

But for that, none of the group by the swimming pool would have had the slightest warning.

He saw a man, perhaps forty yards away.

He saw his hand thrust forward, as at the end of a throw.

He saw a black object, perhaps the size of a tennis ball, coming through the air.

The others saw the alarm which distorted his face. The three guards swung round; one of them had a revolver out in a flash, and fired twice. The roar of the shots was deafening. Two of the guards went racing after the missile-thrower, who was now running at a furious pace, but the girl and Spiro stood as if petrified, looking at the circular object hurtling towards them.

What could it be but a bomb?

After the split second of fear and realisation, Scott thrust the girls aside and ran towards it, hands cupped and close to his body—to make a catch which any cricketer could take comfortably. Everything but the sky and the ball disappeared. It was only two yards away. He could catch it and toss it into the pool, the explosion would be muffled by the water, he ...

He slipped on a patch of wet grass.

He plunged helplessly into the pool as the 'ball' flew over his head. He had a terrible fear of what would follow and, as water struck at his mouth and nostrils, a wild hope that it wasn't lethal, that there was only a message in it. Then, he went under. It was as if his ears were bursting and thunder rolled about him. He had the sense not to struggle, just to hold his breath.

Suddenly, he was hurled bodily out of the water.

He knew what had happened, and the hope died; but he did not see.

One of the guards saw everything.

As Scott skidded off the side of the pool, the ball hit the marble surround. It bounced with a metallic sound. Spiro made an involuntary backward movement, to save himself, then reversed the movement and flung himself at the ball. Before he reached it, there was an explosion which tore his body to pieces; an explosion which turned gold-tanned beauty to crimson horror. In only a split second of time those who had been alive were dead.

Beyond the garden, the one guard who had seen it all stood transfixed; unhurt by flying tiles and pieces of metal.

On the far side of the pool, flung against the handrail, lay Gordon Scott, dazed and only just conscious.

No one came from the house.

From among the trees there came an outburst of revolver fire; a dozen shots each of which sounded like an obscenity in the quiet, for the splashing of the water and the rumbling of the explosion had died away.

A man said: 'Get him.'

'Careful.'

'We won't have to be careful any more. He's dead.'

'Charlie.'

'Yeah?'

'What—what's happened back there?'

Charlie, the man who had watched the three Pentecost girls with such covert attention, made a gulping sound.

'We'd better go see,' he said.

In a few moments, they saw.

And Gordon Scott, dragging himself up right, also saw the dreadful scene.

Soon, one man was helping Scott and the other was going into the house. He made for the nearest telephone and called the Santa Margarita police.

DEATH OF 3 WITNESSES
DEATH OF 3 BEAUTIES
STUDENT CRIMES SPREAD BEYOND CAMPUS
5 DEAD IN BOMB OUTRAGE
MURDERER SHOT DEAD BY POLICE

Gordon Scott, in the office of the Chief of Police at Santa Margarita, read the headlines of newspaper after newspaper and tossed the papers aside. It was three hours since he had returned here from the Pentecost home: after the final, awful scene when Gregory Pentecost came home to find his wife and three daughters dead. Every time he closed his eyes Scott could picture the man's grief. The anguish. The despair.

Now, Gordon was waiting for another witness, the only other witness of the murder of Gerald Lee. He knew her name: Catherine, the murdered man's sister. He had seen her photograph. Now, with two of the local police chiefs, he was going to show her the pictures, and even before she looked at them, she must know that she was a woman in grave danger. Scott had a sudden fear that she would not even get here.

There was a tap at the door, and Spiro's chief said: 'Come in.'

Catherine Lee came in with a policeman just behind her.

The thing which most surprised Scott was her calmness; she did not seem to be under any particular strain. Her hair, nearly black, curled about her neck and ears. She had a pleasantly attractive face, with brown eyes and a rather olive complexion. Much broader and fuller-figured than the Pentecost girls, the way she carried herself was unconsciously seductive. Only when she shook hands with Scott did he realise just how tense she was, how cold her fingers were.

'Miss Lee.'

'I'm glad to know you, Inspector.'

'Miss Lee,' said Spiro's chief, a tall, rangy man who wore a wide-brimmed hat and, most unexpectedly, horn-rimmed spectacles. 'Do you know what happened this afternoon?'

'I know,' Catherine Lee confirmed, and Gordon realised that she had fought hard to win her calmness and was still fighting hard to keep it. There was something about this girl which attracted him, but at that moment he did not think about the attraction, did not even realise that it was there.

'So you know there could be a great deal of danger if you help,' he said. He felt bitterly angry with himself for even thinking of persuading her to help. On the one hand, she was vital to the police case; to an understanding of what was happening throughout the world.

'I know,' she repeated, with that studied calm.

'Miss Lee,' the Chief said. 'Do you recognise either of these men?'

Now, he had larger pictures, almost life-size. Catherine moved closer to his desk and stared down at them. Scott stood stiffly, almost at attention. Her profile was towards Gordon; she had a prominent chin and a straight, well-cut nose.

'I recognise them both,' she stated.

'Where did you see them?'

'On the campus on the night of the riot.'

'What did they do?'

'They molested the Pentecost sisters,' she stated. 'And when my brother tried to stop them, they attacked him too.'

'Just these two?'

'There were four men in all,' she said clearly. 'These were two of them.'

'Would you state that, in court?'

'Yes,' she said. 'Anywhere, at any time.'

The curious thing was that although she spoke with vehemence there was no venom nor, as far as Scott could tell, no bitterness in her voice. She was just flatly positive. Then he remembered how he had been fooled before, realised how much emotion was hiding beneath this calm surface.

The Chief said: 'You've gotta be very careful.' When she didn't answer, he went on: 'You've gotta have police protection everywhere you go.'

It would have been so easy for her to have said, scathingly: 'Like the Pentecost sisters,' but all she did was to nod, apparently in full acceptance.

'Miss Lee,' Gordon Scott said. 'Would you have any objection to leaving this country for a week or two?'

'Not if there was a good reason,' she retorted. Then for the

65

first time, she spoke as if with bitter hurt: 'My parents died years ago. Gerald was my only close relative, I can go any place at any time.'

'We want you to disappear,' said Scott, evenly.

'So that I shall be safe?'

'Yes.'

'Where would you want me to go?'

'Does it matter?' asked Scott.

In his ears Dawlish's voice seemed to be ringing. He had talked to the Deputy Assistant Commissioner by telephone soon after the bombing disaster; and he had spoken to Randy Patton. Both urged him to persuade Catherine Lee to go into hiding. Patton hadn't asked why, and nor had he, Gordon Scott. Patton would be sure that Dawlish had a good reason and he wouldn't demand too much.

'Whom would I go with?' she countered.

'For a start, I'd be your escort.'

'So it would be to England,' she said, slowly.

'Miss Lee,' the Chief said, 'Chief Inspector Scott is a delegate to the International Police Conference. He might want to take you any place—I guess, any place where these guys might be found.'

'That's about right,' agreed Scott. 'I'm under instructions, Miss Lee. And I would be responsible for your safety.'

'Who would be responsible for yours?' she asked.

It was her second flash of bitterness, yet humour lurked in the question. She really was a remarkable young woman. Gordon Scott felt the tug of attraction again, and this time recognised it. This girl's manner, her face, her figure, all combined to attract him. She turned to face him, her eyes as dark as chestnuts just out of their spiky husks. And her gaze as well as her words challenged him. For a few moments he did not know quite what to say, and the Chief fidgeted and breathed hard, reminding him—when he least wanted to be reminded—of Spiro's heavy breathing.

At last he said in a low-pitched voice: 'Miss Lee, if I had my way I would confine you under house arrest, and have the house surrounded so that no harm could possibly come to you.' He moistened his lips. 'I can't do that. But I can tell you you're the most important witness that the police have.' He gulped again, and the Chief nodded sagely. 'This is an international situation. Student unrest is erupting everywhere. And

—and I'm quoting my chief in London now—"the fact that the Pentecost sisters were murdered proves that the conspirators are desperately anxious not to be discovered". So: you are a key which might turn many more locks than those in Santa Margarita.'

All the time she stared at him with growing intensity. What he took to be the calm of self-control in her eyes was really a kind of smouldering fury. When he had finished, she turned to the Chief.

'Do you know of American officers who can confirm what Mr. Scott says?'

'Sure I can. Why, I've been asked by the Sheriff of Los Angeles in person *and* by the F.B.I. to ask you to go with him. This ain't no fake.'

'Do they want me to go now?' she demanded.

'Yes,' answered the Chief. 'They don't even want you to go back home.'

'But my clothes...'

'Plenty of clothes in the shops,' observed the Chief. 'And the government will buy them for you.'

'But my friends!' exclaimed Catherine.

'The authorities don't want anyone to know,' said the Chief. 'And they mean no one.'

'It's crazy!' exclaimed Catherine, momentarily losing self-control. 'I can't possibly! I was going out to dinner this evening with Archie Nemaker, a friend of Gerald's. He...'

'Miss Lee,' interrupted Gordon Scott, 'no one is going to make you come. But if you do, then no one is to know where you're going. And you mustn't give anyone else a chance to follow you. You were followed here, you know.'

'We picked up the guys,' the Chief interpolated smugly.

'It *is* crazy,' Catherine repeated more calmly. 'I don't believe I am the only other witness. There were hundreds of students.' Her voice faltered, as if she had suddenly realised how the other students had melted away at the first sign of trouble. She drew away from the desk and looked out at a car park, used for police cars only. A few men were standing about and talking, all in the same uniform as the Chief. Then suddenly she spun round on Gordon Scott.

'It's monstrous!' she exclaimed. 'It would be like running away! I won't come.'

And she turned and hurried out of the office, where the

guards who had been outside followed her; and when she drove off she had one car escort in front, and one behind. She drove to her home and went inside. There were police and secret service men back and front; everywhere.

They even questioned Archie Nemaker before they allowed him to come in.

Gordon Scott was aware of acute disappointment, much greater than he had real cause to feel. And he could not take his eyes off her. Even when she disappeared, she was still in his mind's eye. It was not, then, that he had any great emotional pull; rather, it was like being mesmerised yet being unaware of it. Certainly he was not afraid.

Into the telephone, an hour later, Dawlish said: 'So she won't go with you Scott.'

'No, sir. She flatly refuses.'

'You must be losing your touch,' Dawlish retorted lightly. 'Stay there, all the same. And whatever you do, don't let anything happen to her.'

'I'm not in charge here,' Scott reminded him quietly. 'I'll do my damnedest but I can't force anyone to do anything.'

'Don't let anything happen to Catherine Lee,' Dawlish insisted, and rang off.

Catherine began to feel twinges of pity for the English policeman. He always seemed to be near the house. The local and the F.B.I. men changed shifts, but Scott seemed to get no rest. He didn't give her any feeling of security; if anything he and the others made her more aware of the danger, although she could not see how anyone could possibly break the cordon. It would be different when she went out, but there was no need to, yet. Tomorrow sometime she would need to go to the market, but not tonight. Archie had left before ten o'clock, fulminating against the police.

His last bitter words had been: 'Kalta may be a trouble-maker and maybe he *is* paid by the Reds, but he's got a case. My God, he's got a case! What do they think we are? A gang of kids?'

He had carried his rage away with him.

Catherine felt only grief and the brush of fear. She was almost fatalistic, and could not explain even to herself why she was so adamant about refusing to do what Gordon Scott had asked.

When she went to bed, he was still outside, as if he meant to sleep at the wheel of his car all night. She looked at him after she had switched off the light in her room and drawn the curtains. The lamplight made him strikingly handsome. The similarity to her dead brother was undoubtedly there but did not affect her. After a while, she went to bed. As she closed her eyes she wondered whether Scott expected an attack on her tonight.

CHAPTER NINE

THE ORDER

A man who sat in the darkness of a big Cadillac spoke into a telephone fitted to his car. He said, quite simply:

'She must go tonight.'

A man in a telephone booth near the campus buildings at Mid-Cal answered:

'Her apartment is bristling with cops, inside and out.'

'Is that a worry for me? She must go.'

The speaker replaced his receiver and touched his chauffeur on the shoulder. The car moved out of the shadows near Fisherman's Quay in San Francisco and rumbled along cobbles and street-car rails before sweeping up and down the hills until he reached a turning near Nob Hill. He got out at one of the houses and went in as the door was opened by a coloured maid. His coloured chauffeur put the car away in a garage nearby and then went into the house by the back entrance. As he waited for the door to open, the lights of the city spread beneath him, the hills carving out great areas of blackness; and along the freeway which crossed the city towards the Golden Gate Bridge, the lights of cars made a tunnel of brilliance in the night.

Kalta put down the telephone.

His eyes were very bright and he looked tired, pale, sick. His lips were set tightly as he walked across a stretch of the Mid-Cal campus towards a wall which had no windows and no doors, and was not guarded by the police. But there was a manhole for water, and it had been enlarged by Kalta and some of the other students so that they could get in and out safely.

He climbed up stone steps into a passage where two students sat reading and watching a window at the far end of the passage, where the police might force an entry. Kalta nodded to them as he turned into the room where the newly formed Students Committee for Action waited. There were seven present; five men and two girls, all watching television. He went across and switched it off.

'We're in business,' he stated.

One of the girls said: 'We're always in business. What do they want now?'

'Cathy Lee.'

'She was always a dead cert,' a man said.

'How?' asked another youth, practically.

It was very strange. They were so calm and matter-of-fact as they stared at Kalta. All of them were first-year students, all were paid agitators, yet had they mixed with the others they looked quite commonplace.

'Her place is crawling with cops,' stated Kalta.

'So was the Pentecost place,' one of the nice-looking youths said.

'Only one way,' said Kalta.

'Blow it up?' the nice-looking student asked, with interest.

'Or set it on fire.'

'Can we?'

'It will be a hell of a risk,' said a man who had not spoken before; he had yellow hair and looked like an angel.

'So there's a risk.'

'So how much do we get?' asked the angelic-looking youth.

'A thousand each,' answered Kalta.

'I'll take the risk,' declared the youth.

'For a thousand, I'd be a human petrol bomb,' said one of the girls. She had pretty eyes and a provocative figure.

'*How?*' asked the youth who seemed to have a one-word vocabulary.

'We drive up to the apartment and when the cops come to question us, throw the bombs at the house,' said Kalta.

'*We.* Is that the royal we?'

'I don't get you.'

'Do *you* appear on the scene, Kalta?'

Kalta said bluffly: 'I've other things to do. Important things.'

'More important than getting yourself blown up for a thousand bucks?'

'I have to be here,' stated Kalta firmly. 'The rest of you draw lots. The thing to remember is that when the job's over

71

you don't come back here. You get lost.'

'How many winners, how many losers?'

'We need four,' Kalta said.

There was a pause, before the pretty girl remarked musingly:

'Two boys and two girls, which makes Susie and me volunteers.'

'It's a good idea,' said Kalta. 'I accept.'

For a few moments, no one spoke. Then one of the men said: 'I don't mind getting lost with Susie.'

'And I'll get lost with any female,' drawled the angelic-faced youth.

'Do we report to H.Q.?' asked Susie, who looked about fifteen, with fair hair dropping to her shoulders, and a tight-fitting sweater moulding a mature figure. She had pretty, pouting lips.

'Yes,' Kalta said.

'When?' asked the man who had so often asked: 'How?'

'Before dawn,' answered Kalta.

'So we don't have much time. Where are the fireworks?'

'In the usual place.'

'Okay,' the man said, and with the youth with the face of an angel and the two girls, went out of the room. When they had been gone for a few minutes, Kalta crossed the room and closed the door. He picked up a copy of *Student Action* and stared down.

It was a quarter-past one.

Catherine Lee slept, so peacefully.

Gordon Scott slept, uneasily, in the back seat of his car. Every now and again, when he woke long enough to shift his position, he wondered:

'Why did Dawlish tell me to stay here day and night? What is he planning to do?'

Dawlish looked down from a helicopter over the sleeping countryside.

There was so much darkness everywhere, but behind, ahead and on his right there were lights, speckling the darkness, whereas to the left was the empty Pacific Ocean, with not even a ship to be seen. Soon, he saw the lights of Santa Margarita, and soon the pilot of the helicopter said:

72

'We aren't far away, now.'

'How far?'

'Five minutes.'

'Are you sure you can get down on the right roof?'

'I couldn't miss it if I tried,' the pilot assured him. 'Can I ask you a question?'

'Yes.'

'Where do we go when we've got the passengers?'

'When we've got the passengers, I'll tell you.'

The pilot laughed.

'You win,' he conceded. 'I know when to shut my mouth.'

There was a lighted patch on the edge of the little town, a floodlit roof, cars with headlights on in the streets surrounding the roof, the shapes of cars. All about were small houses, and one or two larger buildings, obviously new apartment houses. Street lights showed at the corners and along the length of the longer streets; some neon flashed in many colours, drawing the attention of men and women. About a mile away, a car was approaching from the south—from the campus itself. The road was winding and the light streams carved by its headlights shone on trees and on sleeping cattle.

The helicopter hovered over the area of light.

Down below, Catherine stirred in her sleep, and Gordon Scott woke. A man from the sheriff's office came up to his window, and said:

'There's a message for you, Gordon.'

Still half asleep, Scott asked: 'What does it say?'

'You've got to go and try to persuade the girl again.'

'Why, that's crazy!'

'It just sounds British to me,' the sheriff's man retorted. But his smile took away any sting. He opened the door and Scott went straight to the entrance of the apartment house. Two men from the Sheriff's Department were in there.

'Hi, Gordon.'

'Going to wake the babe?'

'Don't stay there too long, buster!'

Gordon Scott waved and grinned and went up in the elevator. When he stepped out at the top landing, the roar of the helicopter was so loud that he was sure it was hovering almost overhead.

My God, he thought. 'It could be an attack. He sprang forward and banged on the door of the girl's room. 'Cathy!

Wake up! Wake up!' Then he realised that she probably could not hear because of the din. He had his key in his hand and thrust it into the lock and turned. As the door swung back, he saw Catherine at the door, obviously terrified; but when she spoke she seemed only to mouth words, for the noise of the engine drowned all other sound.

Then, unbelievingly, Scott heard Dawlish's voice, from behind him.

'Aren't you going to introduce me?' he asked easily.

Gordon saw Catherine stare in utter astonishment. He turned his head and saw Dawlish, who could only have come from the helicopter and in by a fire escape door at the end of the passage. He was utterly incredible. My God! He always got what he wanted.

'Who . . .' began Catherine.

Dawlish said: 'My name is Dawlish. Gordon, go to the helicopter and climb up into the body of it. I shall soon need help.'

And he spoke as if he had no doubt at all that Gordon would obey him.

Outside, the police and the sheriff's men watched the great blade of the helicopter as it whirled above the roof, visible for split seconds at a time. There was no sign of men up there, but a message flashed from a highway patrol car half a mile out on the campus road said:

'A 1968 yellow Chevy is heading your way with four passengers—two male, two female.'

'If they come here,' said the Chief, hungrily, 'we'll pick them up.'

In her apartment. Catherine Lee felt as if this were part of a nightmare, in its way worse then anything that had happened so far. There was the awful din and the light, and now this giant at the door, speaking as if everything was normal. And as he finished speaking, Gordon Scott turned and walked away.

'We're going for a ride,' Dawlish said, with an easy smile. 'Would you care to put on a robe?'

'*I'm* not going anywhere,' she cried.

She saw a change in his expression: a momentary bleakness that was quite frightening. Then, he moved—and she did not think she had ever known a man move with such speed. Her

74

heart leapt into her throat, almost choking her, as he came forward. He seized her, one arm under her knees, one under her shoulder, and lifted her effortlessly. By a sudden shift of position he pressed her face against his shoulder so that she could not scream; even when she tried to bite him her teeth slid over the smooth texture of his jacket. She felt a firm but gentle pressure; firm as a vice but in no way hurting. She tried to kick, but somehow he had rendered even this gesture of hostility impossible.

He carried her; she could see the passage leading to the elevator.

She felt wind first stir and then whip her hair; and on the instant she was cold and felt suffocated, for wind pressed her too tightly against him. And the roaring was so loud it hurt her ears and set her nerves aquiver. She felt someone else touch her, felt herself lifted upwards. Suddenly the fury of the wind stopped and the only thing that disturbed the stillness was nerve-shattering noise; and a fury of shivering.

She thought she heard voices.

She felt herself pressed into a seat, and strapped to it; these were safety belts. She felt the touch of the two men, strangely impersonal, although hands through her flimsy nightdress seemed like flesh touching flesh. She struggled against the belt, but now the giant, sitting next to her, held her hands and she glared at him, mouthing: 'Let me go!'

He smiled back; *smiled*; and kept her in his grip.

She hardly knew why she stopped struggling; perhaps simply because she realised that there was nothing she could do. The door was closed, a curved door shaped like the bulbous cabin of the helicopter. They were already climbing fast. She could see the roof of nearby buildings, the cars in the street, a car coming along the street with its headlights vivid at first and then lost in the bright light which surrounded her building. Dawlish released her.

And then she saw a flash.

It was yellow and red-tinged; and blinded her. She heard a roar. She felt something strike the undercarriage of the helicopter. She began to see again. The pilot and Gordon Scott, in the front seats, were staring down. Dawlish was staring out of his window. There was a strange expression on his face: he looked gaunt and almost skeletal when he glanced up; and then he pointed, out and down. Almost fearfully, she looked out on her side.

A huge fire was now blazing where the apartment house had been. That was all she could see: fire, white and red hot.

She turned back to Dawlish, her eyes stinging with tears. He mouthed some words which might have been: 'It's all right, don't worry.' Then he leaned over the back of his chair and brought forth a poncho, made in a green and yellow tartan. He unzipped this and dropped it over her head and shoulders, then eased her forward with his big and gentle hand, to straighten it behind her. Suddenly, she realised how cold she had been.

She looked down again.

The fire still blazed, but she thought people were moving about, close to it.

If she had been there, she would have been burned alive; and but for this gigantic man by her side, she would have been there. She turned to look at him and saw him holding ear muffs, smiling as he placed the band over her head and the fur pieces over her ears. He was as gentle as a kitten playing; and but for him she would have been dead.

CHAPTER TEN

THE QUIET FLIGHT

Dawlish placed one muff firmly in position but held the other away from Catherine's ear and placed his lips close to her. She felt his warm breath, and heard his deep voice at the same time.

'Be patient. We'll soon be out of this, and you'll have some clothes.'

She nodded.

'Like a sip of brandy?'

She shook her head.

'Just try to rest. I'll explain later.'

Try to rest, she thought bitterly. How could she, how could anyone rest?

The helicopter was turning in a wide circle and it was easier to see the flames and the surrounding houses. Some way off cars were moving fast, red and blue lights flashing. Ambulances, she realised, and fire engines. She leaned back and closed her eyes, at first simply to try to shut the picture out of her mind. She could not. But there were other pictures, too : of Mary, Marie and Maria; of Gerald. Of the wild rioting of the students. Of Archie, so angry with the President of Mid-Cal and the faculty, blaming them for all the trouble. *The fire; Mary, Marie and Maria; Gerald, being surrounded, being kicked to death. Oh God, Gerald. Of the four men, two of whom she had identified from those pictures this afternoon; of Kalta talking, talking, a girl waving a baton—what was her name? Susie, yes, Susie. Of the wild students, rushing. Oh God. Of this huge man by her side, and Gordon Scott.*

Something soothed her.

Perhaps it was the now quieter, rhythmic beat of the engine; or the warmth of the poncho which covered even her knees; or shock; or fatigue. Whatever it was, something soothed her and soon it was not difficult to keep her eyes closed. Before long they felt heavy, and she was only half-aware of noise and movement. She had no idea how long it was before she felt a hand at her shoulder, opened her eyes with a start, and saw Gordon Scott standing by the side of the seat, smiling and saying:

'Wake up, Cathy.'

Wake up.

There was no sound, except that of voices. Dawlish, looking so huge, was talking to another man, perhaps the pilot. There was a big shed, or hangar, with lights and some men inside. And another helicopter and an aircraft. Men were pushing the aircraft. She saw that someone had unfastened her seat belt. Scott backed away but stretched out both arms, to hold her firmly as she stepped out. It was cold, here; sharp cold, very different from any temperature she had known on the coast. Scott held her tightly with one arm, then suddenly exclaimed:

'Fool! Forgot you'd no shoes.'

The cement floor was cold to her feet, but didn't worry her. Suddenly, he picked her up in the same way that Dawlish had done, but with nothing like the same mastery. He had to hitch her high, twice. But he was very sure of himself as he carried her into the big shed, and sat her on a desk.

'Better?'

'I—I'm fine.'

'You've been marvellous!' There was such enthusiasm in his voice.

She thought: I've been a bitch.

'You . . .' she began, but couldn't find words.

'Forget it,' he replied. 'Wait just a moment.'

He had an attractive voice; not so deep as the huge man's but nevertheless very pleasing. And the more she saw of him the more he attracted her. There was something about the way he smiled. He put a finger to his lips.

'Don't move,' he said. 'I'll be back.'

He went across to Dawlish and another man, who were watching one of the small aircraft being pushed out of the hangar, and spoke to Dawlish, who pointed to another corner of the shed. There was a little door, marked: *This is It.* Gordon Scott looked in, then came across to her, picked her up again, and said:

'Clothes over there.'

'Clothes?'

When the great Patrick Dawlish does anything, he does it

properly!'

It was an unpretentious cloakroom, obviously used almost exclusively by men. There were splash stains on the wall behind the handbasin, but the basin itself was clean. Hanging on a hook was a travel bag, and she unzipped this to find a grey coat, a blouse and skirt and jacket, shoes, slippers, underwear. And at the bottom of the bag was a leather purse.

She laughed aloud.

When she checked the size of the clothes, twelves, she was sobered; twelve was her size. The shoes were a little too large. She began to dress, and then heard an engine start up. Were they going in another helicopter? The roar did not prevent her from hearing Gordon Scott call out:

'Have you everything you need?'

'Yes, thank you.'

'Don't be long.'

'I won't be.'

There wasn't much room but she dressed quickly. She opened the purse and found a powder compact, and three different shades of lipstick. She tried one of them, then looked at herself critically in the small wall mirror. It was incredible, but she looked nearly at her best, and the outfit suited her. She went out into the hangar, but no one was nearby. A small jet aircraft was standing some distance away. She could see the stars, very sharp and bright, and the line of hills or mountains in the distance. Suddenly, Dawlish appeared from a doorway marked 'office' in the back of the shed. He stopped at sight of her and raised his hands as if in astonished admiration.

'My! What a transformation!'

She said evenly: 'And what a remarkable fit!'

'I had inside information,' said Dawlish.

'Whom *did* you ask?'

'No one. There is a description of you on our records and it obviously got your measurements right.'

She began: 'But why on earth should . . .' and broke off.

'There's a description of everyone involved in this bad business,' he said soberly. 'Cathy, I'm sorry I acted as I did.'

'Thank God you did,' she said, fervently.

'Gordon told me you had your stubborn moods.'

'Stubborn,' she echoed and laughed. 'Yes. And you couldn't risk leaving me there, could you? Did you know that the house was going to be attacked?'

He hesitated for a moment, before saying:

'Let's get in the aircraft and talk there. We're going to an airfield on the east, so we'll have plenty of time.'

Obviously he took it for granted that she would make no further difficulties, and she did not, although for the first time since they had left Santa Margarita, she felt a moment of resentment at his cavalier behaviour. Then she remembered that but for that, she would be dead. Nevertheless she had mixed feelings about this giant of whom she knew so little. She had none about Gordon, however: when she saw him emerge from the aircraft as they neared it, her heart gave a leap. And his eyes kindled, as he said exactly the same as Dawlish:

'My! What a transformation!'

'And what a remarkable fit,' Dawlish said before she could get the words out. His eyes seemed to be brimming over with good humour, and he gripped Cathy's arm firmly.

'Ask Gordon sometime to tell you how insufferable I am! Ready, Gordon?'

'Yes, sir,' the younger man said. 'Come on, Cathy.'

He led the way up the steps into the aircraft, a ten- or twelve-seater, she saw at once. Soon, she was sitting across a gangway from Gordon Scott, Dawlish behind her. The pilot was visible behind a transparent screen, at the top of which the usual warning lights glowed: *Fasten seat belts. No smoking.* The jet began to taxi, and she was startled at how quickly they were roaring along a runway, and how soon they were up.

Below were the lights of a small town. Over to the left was a star-speckled lake, and obviously a big highway ran to and from the town with a surprising amount of traffic on it. It was as though they had climbed six or seven thousand feet in a second, but in fact the airfield had been on a plateau and once they were off it, they were high above a valley. For a few moments she was content to look down, or ahead at the stars, but at last she turned from the window, and glanced across at Gordon. Again, she was startled: for both he and Dawlish had turned their chairs so that they faced her; and Dawlish leaned forward and touched a button at the side of her arm-rest, and pushed; she was swivelled round so that she faced them in a kind of parlour car.

'This is how millionaires travel,' Dawlish stated. 'Shameful, isn't it?' As he spoke a girl came from the tail-end of the aircraft, carrying a tray with sandwiches and coffee. She put this on a table which fitted into a hole in the aisle floor, and said:

'I'll get the rest.'

'Thanks,' said Dawlish. 'Oh, Letitia—you haven't met Cathy Lee, have you? Cathy, will you say hallo to Detective Sergeant Letitia Cornwall of the Metropolitan Police in London?'

'*Sergeant!*' exclaimed Cathy. 'A policewoman.'

'Hallo, Miss Lee,' the girl smiled. 'Glad to have you aboard.'

'Glad to *be* aboard,' Catherine said huskily. And to herself she added: 'At least I think I am.'

Letitia went off, smart in what looked like an airlines uniform.

'Now, to the question,' Dawlish said briskly. 'No, I didn't know your home was to be attacked. On the other hand the ruthlessness of the previous attacks, one you don't know about as well as that on the Pentecost girls, made it almost certain you would be. I didn't want you to risk staying. But there was no way of making the police officers or the sheriff's deputies force you to go into hiding. However, certain big city police authorities knew the extent of the problem and so did the F.B.I. It's difficult for any State or Federal authority to take the law into their own hands—by kidnapping you, I mean—but it wasn't difficult for them to have certain facilities. I simply took advantage of their generosity.'

'Excuse me, sir,' interrupted Gordon Scott.

Catherine almost understood why he sounded so deferential.

'Yes?' Dawlish encouraged.

'Should you explain that the F.B.I. did warn the authorities at Santa Margarita that if a helicopter came to the building, they should take no action?'

'Oh yes,' agreed Dawlish, and gave his broad, infectious smile. 'The F.B.I. wanted to kidnap you! They certainly smoothed the path. What—ah—does it feel like to be kidnapped?'

Catherine actually laughed.

'I will give you a certificate of efficiency,' she declared; and on the instant, sobered. 'Oh, but it isn't remotely funny. If you'd been a few minutes later . . .' She broke off. 'You say you *didn't* know?'

'Mr. Dawlish has a reputation for seeing into the future,'

interpolated Scott.

'Nonsense!' exclaimed Dawlish, roundly, and she thought he was the most self-confident man she had ever met. 'There is always a sequence of events. In all cases, one event leads to another quite logically. I simply anticipate a series of logical events, and as often as not they occur. As for it being a close shave...' He shrugged. 'We were delayed by mist.'

'Smog,' said the irrepressible Scott.

'Mist or fog over Los Angeles and the foothills,' Dawlish conceded. 'That cost us twenty minutes. And our pilot had to make a detour because of some private aircraft having fun and games near Santa Barbara. So we were half an hour late. If we had been on time, then the explosion and the fire wouldn't have been so close on our heels.'

Catherine said heavily: 'I see.'

'Coffee?' asked Dawlish, as Detective Sergeant Letitia Cornwall came back with another tray of French and Danish pastries.

'Thank you. Mr. Dawlish...'

'Yes?' said Dawlish, pouring coffee.

'Do you know what happened back in Santa Margarita?'

'Yes.' Dawlish said again, very simply. 'Four young people drove up to your apartment house. Your police stood aside, waiting to see what they would do, half-expecting them to try to go up to your apartment. Instead, they tossed high-explosive and fire bombs at the building, and the police were so flabbergasted that the car was able to drive through the cordon before the explosion came. The whole of the building was destroyed,' he went on, bleakly.

'Oh no,' Catherine said brokenly, although what she had already seen had warned her of the extent of the disaster. 'And the residents...'

'Apparently some were lucky and escaped in their night clothes,' Dawlish told her. 'And a ground-floor family of six was away on vacation. All the same, twelve at least died, as well as three policemen and the sheriff.'

Catherine leaned back and closed her eyes.

She heard the clink of cups and saucers; whispering; the sound of coffee being poured, of the protecting paper being taken off a pastry, and yet she was virtually oblivious of these things. The awfulness of what had happened came to her with redoubled force, and slowly, a new factor grew into her mind

82

so that she could think of nothing else.

All these people had died because someone had wanted to kill her.

It seemed utterly incredible, but it must be so.

The death of every man and woman and child in that apartment building was on her conscience; was because of her. It was horrifying; unendurable. Those people would have been alive had she gone with Gordon Scott when he had asked her. She felt her eyes stinging; tears forced their way through the tightly closed lids. She felt one roll down her cheek and rest, as salt, on her lips. She knew it was useless, to feel so badly, yet—she could have prevented this hideous thing.

She felt Dawlish's hand on her shoulder.

'Cathy,' he said. 'If we'd taken you away when Gordon first came for you, those murderers would not have known you had left. There was absolutely nothing you could have done to prevent what happened. Get that into your head, whatever else you do.'

It helped a little; thank God, it helped a little.

She opened her eyes, fumbling for her handbag, but there was a handkerchief in Dawlish's hand, and she took it, dabbed at her eyes, and then blew heavily into it. There was a faint odour of tobacco; somehow, very welcome.

'Thank you,' she said. 'Mr. Dawlish—I'm sorry I was difficult before. I will do anything I can to help, now. Anything at all.'

Dawlish looked at her very steadily. So did Gordon Scott for a few seconds, but as Dawlish began to speak, something made the younger man look away.

Then Dawlish asked: 'Will you help even to the extent of risking your life?'

CHAPTER ELEVEN

LIFE OR DEATH

Catherine was acutely aware of Dawlish's intent gaze; in the cabin light his eyes became a darker blue. She was equally aware of Gordon Scott clenching his hands and gritting his teeth. She was aware, too, of a change in herself. It was as if Dawlish's question had drawn all false thought and emotion out of her; that he was compelling her to see herself and the situation under the searching glare of intellectual floodlights.

She did not at first know the answer.

She knew only that whatever the answer was, it had to be wholly true. The question forced her into heart-searching; into mind-searching; and into a totally unexpected calm.

Neither of the men spoke. About her was the faint, monotonous droning of the two jet engines. A door opened at the far end of the cabin; no doubt that was Letitia. But there were only two soft footfalls, then silence until the door closed again with a faint sough of sound.

At last, Dawlish moved in his chair, relaxing.

'Would you like more time to think about it?' he asked.

With hardly a pause, Cathy replied: 'I think I would like to know more of what you mean.'

'Fair enough,' agreed Dawlish. Full face, he was very strongly handsome. 'Ask any questions you like and I'll try to answer.'

'I would much rather you told me more before I ask questions,' countered Catherine.

'Very well. You know, presumably, that we—that is, the police of many countries—think it possible that the student unrest has a common motivation. That each college may have its own problems, its own resentments and frustrations, but that there may be a single group taking advantage of local conditions.'

When he stopped, she asked: 'You mean, such as world

Communism?'

'Yes. Or world Fascism. Or even a profit motive.'

'Profit?' She was startled. 'How could anyone make a profit out of these uprisings?'

'We don't yet know. We are only dealing in possibilities. The main point is that we believe it possible that there is a single directing intelligence organising the disturbances, taking advantage of local causes of discontent—whether it be racial, or anti-war, or anti-nuclear weapons. *Did* you know we thought this possible?'

'Yes,' Catherine said. 'Gordon told me. Of course every student knows it's a possibility, too. But it wasn't until Gordon talked about it that I took it seriously.' She closed her eyes. 'My brother believed it was Communistic-China inspired.'

'He wasn't alone in thinking that,' remarked Dawlish, 'but it's a long way from proved. Let's move on. It is obvious, isn't it, that something you and the Pentecost sisters saw is causing alarm to the murderers?'

'Surely it's because we could identify the men,' interrupted Catherine.

'It could be that alone,' Dawlish agreed.

'Have you *any* reason for thinking it's more?'

'No reason, except intelligent assumption,' Dawlish answered. 'Of the possibility, I mean. If in fact the cause of the bomb outrage at the Pentecosts' and the outrage at your apartment block is simply because all of you had seen and could identify the men who murdered your brother, then it means that these men could take us direct to their leaders. And that could be the answer although in some ways it doesn't make sense.'

'Why not?' Catherine asked sharply.

'Would the leaders of such an organisation really allow four thugs to have direct access to them? If this were an isolated affair at Santa Margarita, perhaps, yes, but if the trouble at Santa Margarita is part of a global conspiracy, then it's hard to believe your sight of these men is the basic reason for the outrages and the danger to you.'

After a long pause, while she followed all he had said very closely, Catherine asked:

'What other reason could there be?'

'That's what we want to find out.'

'Do you think I might know?'

'It's possible.'

She was stirred almost to anger.

'It isn't even remotely possible. I haven't the faintest idea what is behind this.'

'You could know, nevertheless.'

'Mr. Dawlish,' Catherine said, 'you're not making sense. Either I know or I don't know. It's as simple as that.'

'It isn't, Cathy,' Gordon Scott broke in for the first time since Dawlish had put the vital question to her: 'was she prepared knowingly to risk her life to help the police?'. 'You could know something quite vital without realising its significance.'

She began: 'I don't see how I could possibly...' and then broke off. She was reacting automatically, and not thinking; and she had to think. Now she looked into Gordon's eyes and saw how intent he was, how much it mattered to him that she should understand.

He went on: 'In the case where I first met Mr. Dawlish there was exactly such a situation. A top-ranking New York policeman was under attack and didn't really know why for a long time. When eventually he realised the truth he saw how obvious it was; he simply hadn't understood its significance.'

'You mean,' said Catherine, 'that I may have seen or heard something on the campus?'

'Yes.'

'I suppose you might be right,' she conceded slowly. 'I haven't the faintest idea what it could be though.' She gave a quick, almost brittle, smile. 'I don't think I really believe it's possible but I'll go along with you that it could be.'

Gordon said gruffly: 'That's good.'

'The next step should be a lot easier,' Dawlish went on in his most relaxed manner. 'Obviously, whoever is involved wants to kill you. Obviously, they are fairly numerous and they have access to powerful explosives. Right?'

'Yes.'

'And they will probably try again if they find out where you are.'

'I thought that was why you were so anxious to take me away and hide me,' Catherine said, drily.

Gordon Scott made a little coughing sound. The expression in Dawlish's eyes changed: he was no longer relaxed but tensed up again; and, reflecting his tension, she was suddenly more on edge.

'Yes and no,' said Dawlish.

'Can't you be specific?'

'Yes. We wanted to get you away and out of danger. But we also need you as a bait. We need to place you in a certain position, perhaps in New York, perhaps somewhere else, and let it be known where you are. We think that another attack will then be attempted. We also think that we can protect you and catch your attackers, but we can't catch them until they have shown their hand by attempting to kill you.' He paused, as if to give her time to digest all that he had been saying, then went on in a more casual way: 'Of course we might get other evidence. There are some clues and inevitably other people are involved, but as far as I can judge we are more likely to get to the instigators through you than anyone else. And...' His voice hardened again. 'They are the most ruthless people I have ever come across.'

'And very clever,' put in Gordon Scott.

'And from the way they attacked the apartment house, their adherents are ready to take exceptional risks,' Dawlish continued. 'They could have been blown to smithereens when they threw those fire and high-explosive bombs. Either the incentive is high, or the cause worth dying for.'

Scott said, under his breath: 'Oh, hell! I hate this.'

Dawlish did not even glance at him; and Catherine gave him only a swift, uncomprehending stare before looking back at Dawlish. The droning of the engines seemed even further away. The quiet in the cabin seemed quieter, after that quick eruption from Gordon Scott. Catherine found herself groping for a response. It came suddenly.

'You mean you think they'd *die* for this cause?'

'They seem ready to.'

'But men only die for a *great* cause!'

'That's right,' agreed Dawlish. 'Patriotism, for instance. Even for an ideal, or an ideology.'

'You *really* think these—these agitators feel so deeply?'

'I think they do—or rather, I think they might,' Dawlish answered.

'Then it *must* be Communism.'

'Oh no,' Dawlish said in a tone almost of reproof. 'That's the first careless remark you've let yourself make.'

She was not stung, but the reproof did make her pause; and

pausing, she knew how right he was. This could be Black Power inspired, and many people would die for that. Or it might be anti-black; as many would die for that, too. It might be a kind of anti-Christ; or, if one stretched one's imagination enough, the work of self-appointed apostles carrying the vengeance of the Lord to the people of a world as depraved as Sodom and Gomorrah. Oh, there were plenty of causes for fanatical devotion; and plenty of fanatics to believe in them.

She said quietly: 'Yes. I see. I'm sorry.'

'Catherine Lee,' said Dawlish, stretching forward and covering both her hands with one of his, 'you are a remarkable young woman.'

'You've never said a truer word,' applauded Gordon Scott with great fervour.

'*I* don't think I'm so remarkable,' Catherine objected, almost impatiently. 'But I have always prided myself in being able to think clearly.' She freed her hands and seemed to wave even that thought aside. 'Mr. Dawlish, *do* you really believe the trouble at Mid-Cal is part of a world-wide conspiracy?'

Dawlish hesitated.

'Either you do or you don't,' Catherine said impatiently.

'Cath . . .' began Scott, but stopped.

'Gordon,' said Catherine, with that note of near asperity in her voice, 'I *know* Mr. Dawlish is a very important man *and* your boss, but that dosen't mean that I can't speak plainly to him.'

Scott raised his hands.

'Well, *that's* certainly obvious!'

Dawlish chuckled; and next moment all three of them were laughing; once again he had drawn incipient tension out of the situation. Catherine watched the big man's face and could not fail to see the lines of humour at his eyes and mouth; and when she glanced at Gordon, to see whether he showed any sign of having taken offence, she caught her breath; there was something so wholesome and attractive about him.

'You know, sir,' he said. 'You'll have to answer.'

'Oh, I'll answer,' Dawlish assured him. 'But not until I'm sure I give the right one. Cathy, I nearly told you that I thought it possible that the Mid-Cal trouble is part of a world conspiracy. But that would have been hedging. You made me face a moment of truth, and the truth is that although I can't be sure, I *do* believe it to be so. I do not believe it is simply one of a series of sporadic outbursts; nor do I believe what many people do: that one rebellion triggers off another in a kind of chain-reaction. I think the student revolts across the world are connected: at the very least, that there is a movement or an organisation which immediately takes advantage of incipient unrest; and sometimes actually starts the unrest through students with a predilection for trouble. There are plenty of them hysterical or neurotic enough to be worked up to a state of fanaticism.'

Catherine actually smiled as she responded:

'And the question is, will I die for *my* cause?'

'That's right,' Dawlish said. 'But there's another question you have to answer first.'

'What's that?' asked Catherine.

'Have you *got* a cause?' Dawlish asked simply.

A few minutes ago he had told her that she had compelled him to face a moment of truth; and now, he had forced her to the same crisis. *Had* she a cause? She had a deep, burning hatred for the men who had beaten her brother to death, but was seeking them out for vengeance a cause? Would she be prepared to die so that his murderers could be caught? The moment she posed the question she knew that to die simply for vengeance, even to avenge her so-loved Gerald, was not in her heart. And she had liked Mary, Marie and Maria but she would rather live than face serious risk of death to avenge them.

Dawlish's question was so much wider in concept.

Did she care about what was happening at Mid-Cal?

She had been very young when there had been such a surge of movement among students for McCarthy in his struggle for the Democratic Party nomination for the Presidency, but she had been fiercely in favour of it. And Gerald, two years older, had been a tremendous supporter of the Senator. So had Archie Nemaker.

Freedom *did* matter to her.

So did such causes as integration and civil rights; the anti-poverty programme. And it mattered to her that people of whatever race and religion and age and political beliefs should be able to fight for what they believed. She did *not* believe in intimidation. It was intimidation in Czechoslovakia in 1968 which had first fired her to indignation. She hated war and the rule of force and tyranny and violence . . .

Very quickly, and very sure of herself, she answered Dawlish.

'Yes,' she said. 'I have a cause.'

'Can you tell me what it is?'

'The rights of man,' she answered, and the old, old phrase did not sound glib, because it was exactly what she meant.

'That's everything,' said Dawlish with great strength of feeling. 'It's the one cause which espouses all causes as I see them. Will you take your chance of dying for the cause?'

'Yes,' she answered. 'But . . .'

Gordon Scott was leaning forward on the edge of his chair, and there was a sudden dimming of the radiance in his eyes.

'But?' echoed Dawlish.

'I don't want to throw my life away,' Catherine explained with simple forthrightness. 'I would like to think I had a good chance of helping to get results and of surviving. Isn't *that* reasonable?'

Dawlish stared; and then gave a deep chuckle of laughter. He sprang up from his chair and drew her up from hers, and gave her a bear-hug which seemed powerful enough to crush her bones but did not hurt at all, in fact gave her a feeling of great security and comfort.

He stood back, at last.

'I for one will fight for your life, my honey! And if I'm not mistaken, there is another.'

He looked at Gordon Scott.

Catherine was aware of a subtle change in the mood of the two men. It was as if for a few moments her response had exhilarated them. Now they were facing two realities. She was not affected, for she had faced the realities before she had spoken. It would never enter her head to go back on her undertaking now. These two could not know that, but they would gradually find out.

But in one way her mood did change.

She looked at Gordon and saw the expression, the near-longing, in his eyes; and her heart began to beat faster. She forgot Dawlish. There was only Gordon here with her, only he mattered. Was he trying to tell her that he felt the same?

It was Dawlish who broke the silence.

'We ought to have a nap,' he said. 'I'll take a chair at the back—they can be very comfortable. Don't stay up too late, you two.'

CHAPTER TWELVE

DILEMMA

Dawlish, behind them, was breathing very heavily; almost snoring.

Gordon, by her side, was looking at her; there was just enough light to show that his eyes were open. Yet he hadn't spoken since they had put the reclining chairs back close together.

His hand was on hers.

She had expected him to say what he felt. True, he might be inhibited by Dawlish, but Dawlish wouldn't be able to hear if they spoke in whispers. And she needed to talk; needed the reassurance that he was interested in her for herself, and not simply because she was ready to fight for a cause. Yet they had been here for fifteen or twenty minutes.

What *was* on his mind?

Had he already got what he wanted from her? Was he policeman first and man a long way afterwards? From what she had seen, this didn't seem possible, but—old cliché—you never could tell with men. Perhaps—ah!—perhaps it was because he was British. Perhaps the British, well, the English, *were* more reticent and shy than Americans. Could he possibly be thinking that if he talked about—well, if he talked as man to woman—she would think that he was taking advantage of the situation? Whatever it was, obviously he wasn't going to broach any subject.

Should she?

Oh, nonsense! If he wasn't interested in her, what was there she could do? Perhaps she had misread the signs. Much of her life on the campus was fending off admirers, would-be lovers, some of whom thought that any girl was an easy lay if they only set their minds to conquest. What on earth was the matter with her that she could even contemplate talking to him?

Dawlish's heavy breathing turned into a snore. Then there was a rustling, as if he had turned over, and silence fell. Even the droning of the engines now seemed a part of living; not simply noise, any more than the beating of her heart was noise.

She closed her eyes.

'Cath,' Gordon whispered.

Instantly, she opened her eyes wide and turned her head.

'Yes, Gordon?'

'You—you're very beautiful.'

'Thank you,' she said; and her heart leapt.

'You—you really are. And...'

He broke off, and she did not speak or move, but waited with her heart now beating fast.

'... very brave,' he said.

'Not brave,' she whispered. 'I feel afraid. That's if I feel anything.'

'That's the truest bravery,' he said. 'Facing danger and wishing you could turn and run away.' He caught his breath. 'Danger.'

'Gordon,' she said, 'don't worry about me.'

'Not worry about *you*!' His voice was suddenly almost loud.

'*Hush!*' she breathed.

'Sorry,' he said. 'I...' He broke off.

What was it he couldn't bring himself to say? That his heart beat fast for her, that he was as aware of her closeness as she was of his? Didn't he realise that in such a situation as this emotions could grow fast, that everything that had taken place since they had met had quickened every kind of perception? Surely...

'Cath.'

'Yes?'

'I...'

But still he could not finish what he wanted to say. There was silence and stillness in the cabin. She wanted to move towards him, to touch, to hold, to be held. Yet she must not be overbold. He *was* English. He...

'Oh hell!' he breathed.

And as the words came out he thrust the arm of his chair up, so that there was nothing between them. And suddenly his hands were upon her, and she was responding to a passion he had been stifling. His hands; his lips. In those moments there was a writing of bodies, hands upon breasts, upon flesh, lips hot as they met, tongues at first cool and then warm as if their very selves were merging, entering. Time, as they were aware

92

of time, stood still.

And they were one.

And soon they were breathless and yet still.

And soon they were caressing, and gentle, all passion spent but their need of each other as deep as before.

He said: 'Are you comfy?'

'Yes.'

'Think you can sleep?'

'Yes.'

'Like a blanket over you?'

'Perhaps—perhaps we'd better.'

So, he pulled the blanket up and they were snug and warm, and they slept.

Dawlish woke, to see daylight coming in at the windows which had not been covered the night before. He was stiff but rested, and although his great body overlapped on both sides of one chair, and his legs were on another, he did not feel too uncomfortable. He dozed for a while. Then he began to think. If it was daylight then they had been flying for at least five hours—probably six. Where were they? And how long would it be before they landed?

How were the others?

Squinting along the cabin, he could see the top of Scott's head and the tips of Catherine's feet. They must be sharing a seat. Hmm. He sat up. From here he could see more: enough to show that in fact they were in two of the seats but pretty well as close together as they could get. *Hm-mmm.* He wanted to go along to the loo and he wanted a cup of tea and he wanted to know what they were going to do about landing. But he did not want to disturb the couple a moment earlier than he had to.

He made as little noise as he could when getting up and walking along the cabin. It was nonsense to pretend to avert his gaze, to pretend that he didn't see. A blanket covered them up the waist, but Catherine's blouse was draped over her shoulders, and there was no sign of her bra. *Harrumphh!* He went to the partition and pushed it aside, to see Letitia at the tiny galley, a kettle boiling, toast made and two trays ready.

She looked up brightly. She was auburn-haired, pleasant-looking, with a pleasing but not obtrusive figure; she wore her uniform skirt, and a shirt blouse of pale blue.

'Good morning, sir!'

'Good morning. Sleep well?'

'Very well.'

'Good. Is that tea for me?'

'It was for the pilot, but I can make him some more.' She poured out.

'Ah ... Thanks.' He sipped. 'Wonderful! Don't know what I'd do without my morning cuppa.'

'Nor do I.'

'Are you in the pilot's confidence?' he asked.

'If you mean when are we going to land at Vadife—in about an hour, sir.'

'Nice time. Did we go as fast as we hoped?'

'We'll have an hour in hand.'

'Splendid! Any radio messages, do you know?'

'Reports from Santa Margarita, sir. That's all, as far as I know.'

'Good? Bad? Indifferent?'

'Eleven died last night,' Letitia told him quietly.

'Oh.' He finished his tea. 'Bad,' he said, 'dreadful.'

'The police and National Guard made an attempt to get into the university building,' she volunteered.

'Failure?' asked Dawlish.

'Two guardsmen were shot, sir.'

'*Shot!*'

'It does make you wonder whether we're dealing with students or revolutionaries, doesn't it?'

'Need there be a difference?' Dawlish asked.

'I suppose I shouldn't ask what *you* think, sir,' she countered.

'You may ask. And I will tell you that I don't know what to think. No other messages, then?' His manner was more staccato than usual, partly because of the couple a few yards away.

'There will be a summary from Chief Inspector Sills when we reach Vadife,' Detective Sergeant Letitia told him.

'Good for Sills. Ever struck you how dependent we are on others, Letitia?'

'*You* don't feel like that, surely?' She sounded shocked.

'Don't you believe it. Just at the moment I'm very dependent on you. I want some kind of noise made, or a waking device, so that Chief Inspector Scott can wake, as he believes, of his own accord. If you know what I mean.'

Her eyes were dancing.

'I know exactly what you mean.'

'Good. How will you arrange it?'

'If you will go back to your seat, sir, and settle down as if you haven't yet been awake I will use the loud-speaker system. I'll say we're getting ready to land, or—well, something.'

'Very resourceful,' approved Dawlish. He beamed. 'Now to make that very convincing you could take them some tea—orange juice might be better for Miss Lee—and me, too. I don't know what I should do without my second cup of morning tea, do you?'

'If you ask me, sir,' said Letitia, with obvious admiration, 'I think you could cope with almost any situation.'

'So we have acquired a mutual respect,' Dawlish said. 'Dare I steal a minute or two to wash, do you think?'

'I can take the pilot's tea in now, if you do,' replied Detective Sergeant Cornwall.

'Do just that,' approved Dawlish. 'Then everything in the garden will be lovely.'

But would it be, for Dodie Patton? According to Patton she was in love with Gordon Scott, and a weekly letter seemed evidence that he returned the affection. Did he? Dawlish was as sure as he could be that Gordon was not a womaniser, but he wasn't behaving with Cathy as if he was in love with another woman. She seemed to have mesmerised him.

Well, it was none of his business. Was it?

He washed and used an electric razor, then passed the sleeping couple again, going back, as it were, to bed. Very soon, there was a squeaking and squawking over the loudspeaker, followed by the detective sergeant's voice, much louder than it need be, even startling him. He heard movements, a gasp or two, more movements, and then another announcement, as if this were a commercial flight.

'For anyone who is interested we are flying close to the north coast of Brazil, and we shall begin to descend half an hour from now, to land at Vadife, which is between Recife and Salvador.'

Into the silence which followed, Dawlish let out a gargantuan yawn, stretching his enormous arms and legs as if he were just waking. Gordon Scott stood up, fastening his shirt collar. He looked tousled and attractive, and sounded a little over-hearty.

'Sleep well, sir?'

'As the just,' boomed Dawlish. 'And you? ... And ...'

A few minutes later, Letitia brought three trays, neatly balanced on top of one another. Catherine bobbed up. Dawlish, with his hyper-sensitive powers of observation, was quite sure that she was much less affected than Gordon Scott, who was a little over-loud, over-solicitous. After a glass of orange juice, she disappeared. Almost as soon as she had gone, Gordon approached Dawlish. He came obviously with his mind set, and Dawlish tried to imagine what he was going to say. He, more than anyone else, was aware of how deeply committed the younger man had been—in fact was—to Dodie Patton.

'Excuse me, sir.' He was pale and unshaven and a little dark under the eyes.

'Yes, Gordon?'

'Have you made any decision about—about our next move?'

'Yes. Unless there's a very strong reason against it, waiting for us in Vadife, I shall send you ahead to Golana with Cathy. She'll be much safer there than in most places and easier to protect. I'll have more advance guards out there to help you watch, and she will probably get a kick out of helping with preparations for the conference. I think she's wholly trustworthy, so you can tell her anything you like about what we're doing. If she should prove unreliable then you and others will soon see indications: just one attempt to telephone outside Golana, for instance, or one telegram or letter, could give her away. But I repeat, I think she's trustworthy.'

'So do I, sir,' Scott said. 'But ...' He hesitated, and coloured. Then he burst out: 'Can you find me some assignment back home, sir? Or in New York?'

Dawlish considered him very thoughtfully, having no doubt of the intensity of his feelings but some doubt of what caused them.

'Gordon,' he said reassuringly, 'if you think I'm simply sending you to spy on Cathy Lee, forget it. I want you to look after her. I don't know anyone whom I could rely on more for that.'

Scott seemed to set his jaw.

'It isn't that, sir.'

'Then what is it?' Dawlish was compelled to ask bluntly. 'There *is* a job to be done.'

'I know, sir. And in a way I would give my right arm for the chance. But—well, I've strong personal reasons, sir.' When Dawlish simply stared at him he coloured more deeply and gulped in obvious confusion. 'I know that there's no justification in allowing private affairs to interfere with one's work, sir, but—well, if it's possible, I think they should be taken into account.'

'So do I,' said Dawlish, and went on as if obtusely: 'What's on your mind, Gordon?'

'I've run into something I've never run into before,' Gordon Scott answered. 'I'm not sure that I can trust myself.'

Dawlish said mildly: 'Perhaps you had better tell me.'

Scott glanced beyond Dawlish but there was still no sign of Catherine. He said nervously, gaining more confidence as he went on:

'You know I'm engaged to Dodie Patton, don't you?'

'I had heard of it,' Dawlish said.

'Until I went to Santa Margarita it hadn't occurred to me that I would look twice at another girl,' stated Scott simply. 'But I hadn't been with Cathy long before I fell absolutely head over heels. She's so different from Dodie, but—oh, what the hell! I simply can't keep my mind on the job if I'm with her. Apart from the emotional involvement, there—there's a kind of guilt complex about Dodie. I feel—well, I—er—I—er—I know this must sound dreadfully callow, sir, and I'm damned sorry. But if you've taught me anything, it's that to do this job properly you have to be one hundred per cent on the job. And I honestly don't think I can be.'

He stopped and stood like a guilty schoolboy in front of a stern master. He was comparatively young, of course, but he must be in the thirties. With one part of his mind Dawlish marvelled at his lack of sophistication; with the other he felt both sorry and a little impatient. But impatience could be controlled. Here was a man with an acute personal problem, and there was no one but Dawlish to whom he could turn for any kind of help.

Yet Dawlish had to keep his mind one hundred per cent on the task of finding the cause of worldwide unrest.

At that moment, Catherine appeared from the washroom.

CHAPTER THIRTEEN

COMPUTER-MIND

She looked quite lovely.

She was made up slightly, her hair brushed to a dark sheen. She was bright-eyed, her rumpled blouse hidden by a light-weight jacket slung over her shoulders. In a way she looked younger, and Dawlish realised that until this morning her expression, caused by grief and anxiety, had made her seem much older than she was.

Now, she was—radiant.

And young Scott looked at her as if no other woman existed; whatever his misgivings, her presence drove away everything but awareness of her.

If she sensed that anything was wrong, she did not show it.

'Planning your next dangerous move?' she asked, lightly.

Dawlish thought: There isn't any doubt at all. She's fallen in love with him. Aloud, he said: 'Our next move is to land at Vadife and then fly from there to Gola.'

'*Where?*' She was startled.

'Gola, the capital of Golana.'

'You mean the Central African state?'

'Yes.'

'Good grief!' she exclaimed. 'Why?'

'Representatives of all the world's major police forces will meet here next week,' Dawlish told her. 'And each one will have an up-to-the-minute report on the position of campus or university troubles in his country. Every university where there is trouble or the threat of trouble is being closely watched by the police.'

'Good grief!' she exclaimed again. 'Was Mid-Cal?'

'Yes. Our chief agent, an F.B.I. man, was murdered. The two men you've recognised from the Identikit pictures are suspected of murdering him. So! We go to Golana. I shall fly back to London for consultations, you and Gordon will be on the spot where he will be helping the local police and administrators to get ready for the conference. Convention,' he added quickly.

She could have asked: Why send *me* there?

She could have protested that he had no right to send her to Golana.

All she did was to put a hand on Gordon Scott's arm and say with obvious excitement:

'I've always wanted to go to Africa!' She stared into his face and then at Dawlish. Slowly, the excitement began to fade but the radiance did not go entirely. 'I suppose I'm being very callous,' she went on, 'but I *am* excited about it, and now that I'm away from Santa Margarita everything that happened seems like a bad dream. Please don't disapprove of me too much.'

'The trouble with you is that as soon as you start behaving normally, you are seized with a guilt complex,' said Dawlish lightly. 'You can't live forever in grief. One has to come up to the surface.' He looked out of a window. 'Our next plane is due to leave at twelve noon. There'll be just time to have a quick look round. We'll find a policeman to take you. Gordon and I have to be busy.'

'If I don't hurry, I won't have time to shave!' Gordon said, and he hurried towards the washroom.

It was very hot and humid. There was no breath of wind, and the sea looked like glass, while the palms and the banana trees were a curious yellow-green colour. Here and there were huge splashes of scarlet bougainvillaea. The sky was a pale blue, and the sun stung. All of these things were obvious as they walked from the aircraft to a small airport building, led by police and customs officials. They stepped inside the building —and into blessed coolness. A middle-aged man with silver-grey hair, wearing a pale blue uniform, beautifully cut, came forward to welcome Dawlish.

'I am Commissioner Junta,' he announced in excellent English. 'It is a great pleasure to meet you, Major Dawlish.'

They shook hands, were introduced, passed through customs without formality. At the office was a temporary identification certificate for Catherine, which would serve as her passport on this particular series of journeys. A youthful officer, also in the uniform of what proved to be the *Garda Civile*, looked delighted at the chance of carrying Catherine off in an air-conditioned Chevrolet. Dawlish and Scott were taken to an office where at least a hundred different reports were laid out on a vast desk. By the desk stood a grey-haired woman. She was big and unprepossessing, but there was a tremendous vitality about her.

'Miss Camilla Felísta,' Junta introduced. 'She has been in charge of opening and sorting all reports, and of taking messages from your office, Major. She is of course beyond all doubt trustworthy. And efficient.'

Camilla Felista smiled, her huge teeth flashing.

'And is at your service,' went on Junta.

'You're very kind,' Dawlish said. He had envisaged having to go through all the reports while flying the South Atlantic, but it would be a great help if he could make a start here. 'If I can make notes on each report and if Miss Felista can send replies by cable, telephone or teletype...'

'All facilities are next door,' she interpolated, also in good English. 'There I have the confidential assistants. We have two and one quarter hours. We begin?'

Dawlish said mildly: 'We can't begin soon enough. Inspector...' He turned to Gordon Scott. 'Will you...'

'Major,' interrupted Miss Felista, 'to save time I have sorted the messages into three kinds.' She pointed to three batches of reports, placed like a ladder one on top of the other. At the top left-hand corner of each was the name of the country from which the report came, printed in a bold hand it was easy to pick out on the instant. She placed a beautifully shaped and manicured finger on the right-hand letters. 'These, if you please, are urgent, concerning upheavals already outbreaking in certain universities. These'—her finger shifted—'are about the inquiries you made yourself and are being made at the Mid-Cal, yes. *These*...' She shifted her finger again. 'These are reports of the way in which the trouble is being planned.' She caught her breath, and then as Dawlish opened his mouth to thank her, she let out a great gust of breath, and her brown eyes positively glistened with triumph as she picked up a puce-coloured folder from the desk. 'Here is *my* report. The summary. Please to consider.'

Dawlish said: 'You are a tremendous help, and very kind.'

'It is not my being kind that matters,' declared Camilla

Felista. 'It is am I being of good service?'

Dawlish said: 'Will you give me ten minutes on my own, please, to consider?'

'As you wish,' she said, 'but perhaps better if I explain ...'

He gave her a friendly smile, but his voice was quite un-yielding.

'I will ask for your explanations later.'

'*You* are kind,' she said, stiffly. She shut her mouth, her teeth appearing to snap together, then flounced through a doorway leading to the other office, moving with quite remarkable grace.

'She is a most efficient woman,' Junta said. 'Now, please, excuse me. Please ask for any help you wish.' There was a twinkle in his eyes as he turned to the door. As it closed behind him, Scott said:

'Wow! She thinks she's tops.'

'Let's find out if she is,' said Dawlish. 'Skim through the Yard reports and put aside any that want immediate action.' He opened the folder, and for a moment was puzzled, for there were graphs and there were columns of typewritten figures; for that moment it was almost as if he had been given the wrong file.

But he hadn't.

With a mind which must be like a computer, Camilla Felista had evidently been meticulously through the reports. Then she had drawn up headings, such as:

Number of 1st-Year Student Trouble-makers	Suspected Professional Agitators	Number of known drug addicts	Cause of Grievances (i.e.: racial facilities)	Number of established students sympathetic to trouble-makers	Proportion of established students sympathetic to total college population

On the left hand column was the name of the college, the Principal or President, and the country or state. Gradually a comprehensive picture of the situation throughout the world emerged, and Dawlish sat back, astounded.

'Have a look at these,' he said to Gordon.

'Right, sir. There are half a dozen reports which need prompt replies.'

'Let me see.' Dawlish stretched out for them.

101

He scanned the reports, all from Sills, in London. For each delegate at the convention the Golana authorities wanted £10 a day for full board and lodging, 'entertainments', free facilities with taxis, public transport. Did Dawlish agree that this was reasonable? He marked the sheet: *Very*, and turned to the next. Several delegates wanted to know whether the purpose of the convention should be publicised or whether the agenda should mislead. Dawlish wrote: *I think we should now publicise true reasons*, and put that aside. The next asked: Do we want academic lecturers at the convention, and university administrators, or should this be exclusively police? Dawlish hesitated, and then wrote: *Exclusively police unless there is a world-wide authority.* If there were, he had never heard of one. Then came a vital question: Will four days be long enough; isn't a week needed? from several delegates. Dawlish wrote: *Make facilities for a week but finish earlier if possible.* There was a personal note from Sills: Mrs. Dawlish telephoned. You have a family engagement for Sunday. Shall she cancel? He wrote: *Not yet.* For Sunday was five days away. Finally there was a note from Van Woelden: Will you be chairman of this convention and can we include on the agenda the advisability of establishing a full-time professional secretariat? Dawlish hardly paused to ponder before he wrote; *Much rather you be chairman, anyone but me. Yes to secretariat.* The truth was that he had been virtually bundled into the job of convenor and organiser of the conference and the last thing he wanted to become was an administrator.

He drew back from the desk.

'She is remarkable,' Scott announced. 'Camilla Felista, I mean.'

'Yes,' agreed Dawlish. 'Ask her to come in, will you?'

She came in much more sedately than she had gone out; she had powdered her cheeks, and put a red rose in her hair. There was a look of expectancy about her as she approached Dawlish. He studied her very closely.

'Senhor Dawlish has questions to ask me?' Her voice was stiff.

'I'd appreciate some help,' Dawlish said. 'At how many of the colleges, you have entered is drug-addiction a serious problem?'

'Fifty-one out of a total of one hundred and twenty-seven,' she answered. 'In the United States and in Japan the addiction

102

is most serious, the proportion being . . .'

'Thank you. What is the most common form of drug used?'

'In everywhere, L.S.D. or marihuana, otherwise cannabis,' she answered promptly. 'In twenty-four colleges heroin is of the serious nature.'

'In how many of the colleges have weapons—guns, rifles, shot-guns—been used by the students in revolt?'

'Thirty-eight, but also seven more have used the smoke-bomb, the petrol bomb and the knife.'

'How many causes of student grievances are there?'

'I have not attempted always to distinguish, she answered, without the slightest hesitation. 'In the United States racialism is in nearly every case but in all there is a variety. There had not been the time for me to make the full analysis but if you wish for it, senhor, I could study the figures and perhaps be finished before you leave for Golana.'

Dawlish looked at her very thoughtfully, an idea growing fast in his mind. She began to frown, and frowning, she looked remarkably like a frog; but her brown eyes glowed with intelligence.

'Miss Felista,' he said, at last, 'would it be possible for you to take leave of absence from your duties here?'

'For how long?' she flashed.

'Perhaps three months,' he answered.

Her eyes began to dance.

'For what purpose, senhor?'

'You have a remarkable grasp of statistics, and the situation as a whole. I doubt if anyone else could help so well to keep records of all the statements and the speeches made at the convention. Clearly it will take a lot of time . . .'

'Who would, please, employ me and be responsible for the salary and expenses?'

Dawlish answered slowly: 'I think the conference would agree to appoint a secretariat, and the secretariat would be responsible,' Dawlish said. 'If that didn't work out, I would be responsible.'

'*You!*' Her eyes now flashed. 'In your private capacity?'

'I would guarantee to meet the cost if there were difficulties from the police authorities,' Dawlish said.

She stood very close to him. He could hear her heavy breathing, and could see the rise and fall of her breast. The odd thing was that there were tears in her eyes, and her lips

103

quivered. He was half-afraid that she would fling her arms around him. But without a second's warning she pirouetted and then whisked herself away from him, saying:

'I will make the inquiry. Thank you.'

She flung herself out of the room, and it was as if a whirlwind had suddenly dissipated into calm air.

Dawlish sat back, ruefully smoothing his hair, and Gordon Scott leaned against the desk, looking much more himself than he had for two or three days. He actually chuckled.

'She really is something,' he said. 'And she's got a mind like a computer. You know what will happen if . . .' He broke off, suddenly, as if embarrassed. 'I mean, she might not mix well with some of our more phlegmatic northern Europeans!'

'That's true enough,' Dawlish said. He wondered what Scott had started out to say, then put it out of his mind. 'All the reports are summarised, and I needn't read them until we're on the aircraft. I wouldn't mind a bath and a good meal, either. How about you?'

'That goes for me, too,' Scott said.

They telephoned Junta, who said simply: 'It is no trouble. My apartment is at your disposal. I shall send a car for you. And while we are speaking, Major, Camilla Felista has made application for what is I believe known as leave of absence. I have personally approved this, and sent it to the Security Minister who I expect will also approve.'

'You're very good,' murmured Dawlish.

'For her it will be a great opportunity,' said Junta. 'For me, a great loss.' There was a pause before he said: 'In ten minutes . . .'

He broke off.

Dawlish heard the catch of his breath, and heard him say in Portuguese: 'What is it?' There was a gabble of voices and Dawlish could not distinguish one word from another, until Junta's voice sounded in his ear again.

'There has been an attack on Miss Lee,' stated the Brazilian. 'She has been injured.' And the words echoed clearly from the earpiece so that Scott, already startled by the change in Dawlish's expression, heard the words. Dawlish, badly shaken, saw the change on Scott's face, and if he had needed any more telling, now knew beyond doubt how the other felt about Catherine Lee. His own voice was clear but low-pitched as he asked:

'How badly is she hurt?'

'I am awaiting news,' said Junta. 'And every policeman in Vadife is looking for her assailant. Major—one thing is now obvious, perhaps of more importance. You were traced here.'

CHAPTER FOURTEEN

NEAR MISS

Being driven about the island, up into the foothills through lush grass and bush-land, seeing the glow of the volcano in the distance, being shown the main street with its few exotic shops, the near-white sand of the beaches with their fringe of palms, Catherine felt more content than she had for a long time. She was aware of the lively, likeable, mustachio'd officer's admiration, although he was punctiliously formal. The white buildings, the bougainvillaea, the unbelievably blue-green grass, were reminiscent of parts of Southern California, and not unlike a miniature Palm Beach. She wished Gordon were here with her, but every now and again she hugged herself because of the prospect of going to Golana. As often, she was astounded at her own reactions. She had dated frequently enough, she was fond of Archie, but she had never even begun to feel like this.

There was very little traffic.

Most of the people about were Europeans, but many looked much more Mexican or Spanish. The men were nearly all stripped to the waist, and remarkably tanned. The women wore short, colourful dresses, almost like squaw dresses in North America. Most of the cars were large, new and American, but she saw two Rolls-Royces, some M.G.s and several Japanese Toyotas. Their chauffeur-driven car turned into one of the beaches, towards a white building, dazzling in the sun.

'We will go to there, the most exclusive club in Vadife, for a drink,' said her guide.

A small Toyota saloon which had just passed them swung suddenly into the beach road, forcing their chauffeur to jam his brakes. The small car pulled into the side. The chauffeur glowered as he started off again. Catherine caught a glimpse of a man in the back of the Toyota, and another at the wheel.

'Such fools,' her escort condemned angrily, but when they

stopped at the entrance to the club, he was all smiles and courtesy again. He got out first and handed her down.

No one would ever know what made him glance towards the Toyota.

Catherine saw the change in his expression and felt him snatch at her hands and pulled her to him, a surprisingly powerful bear-hug for so small a man. There was a sharp rattle of shooting; she saw the man at the back of the Toyota pointing the gun towards her. She heard the *clucking* sounds as bullets buried themselves in her escort's back. She did not fully realise what had happened, but felt him begin to sag; she was actually holding him up. Next moment she felt a blow at the side of her head, and on the instant lost consciousness.

As she fell, a police car which had been following the 'tourists' all the time, swung into the beach road. The driver of the little car ducked out of sight. The passenger made no attempt to save himself, and bullets riddled his chest.

'How is she?' Scott barked.

'She is not badly hurt,' said Junta.

'Where is she, please?'

'She is in the club house, and a doctor is with her. She will have the best of attention, I assure you.'

'Can we be sure she is safe?' Scott demanded.

'The man who shot her is dead,' said Junta. 'He arrived on the morning aircraft from Mexico City. He was alone. He had a Russian automatic rifle. We do not have reason to believe there will be other attacks but rest assured that Miss Lee will be protected.'

They were in the office where Dawlish had studied the reports and Camilla Felista's summary of the reports. Dawlish was in the other room, telephoning London, and Camilla was at a switchboard, getting the call. Scott felt almost sick from the shock of what had happened. He knew that he was being too aggressive, and yet was finding it very difficult to speak calmly. He was biting on a temptation to retort that Junta's men had not made a very good job of protecting Catherine so far, when Dawlish came in.

He said: 'I've just heard about the lieutenant who died protecting Miss Lee. I am desperately sorry, Colonel.'

'He was doing what he had to do,' Junta said sharply.

'Exactly what happened?' Scott asked.

'He protected Cathy with his body,' Dawlish said from the door. 'I'm told he had eleven bullets in his back.' There was a long pause, before he went on: 'I've sent all the replies to London. Unless something else comes in, we're through with the job. Can we have lunch at this club, Colonel, instead of accepting your very kind offer?'

'It is perhaps better,' answered Junta. 'We shall not have to move her twice. Major Dawlish . . .'

'Yes, Colonel?'

'It is possible there is another attacker here.'

'Yes,' Dawlish said. 'It wouldn't be surprising.'

'Excuse me, sir,' said Gordon Scott, 'but shouldn't I be over at the club with Miss Lee?'

'That's where we're going,' Dawlish reminded him. 'Go and see how Camilla is getting on, will you?' Scott went out and Dawlish continued: 'Colonel . . .'

'Major?'

'Is there a university or a university college on the island?'

'No,' answered Junta promptly. 'But there is a convalescent home for university students only. Do you think it possible that one of the students there might receive instructions to do what the dead man failed to do?'

'Obviously it is possible,' Dawlish said.

'I will arrange for the home to be closely guarded,' Junta promised. 'And I will find out if any long-distance telephone calls have been received.' He looked very tired as he turned towards the door, and his movements were slow. 'Major, you see the significance of your suspicion, don't you?'

'Yes,' said Dawlish. 'Wherever there is a college there could be a killer. If . . .' He broke off. 'It's only guesswork,' he added gruffly. 'But if there is one potential assassin in a little place like Vadife, then there could be many in every town and city which has a university.'

'We shall find out,' said Junta, with a show of confidence. 'Your aircraft will leave in two hours from now, I am assured.'

'You're very good,' said Dawlish, and he went across and opened the door for the colonel.

Gordon Scott was already at the desk, checking the reports against Camilla's summaries. Dawlish watched him, moodily. With his personal involvement and dilemma, Scott was under a great deal of pressure, and the way he reacted would be clear indication of his quality. In the past he had shown great physi-

108

cal courage; he was astute as well as intelligent; and he never gave up. He had never married, and as far as Dawlish had been able to find out, before meeting Dodie Patton, had had no serious *affaire* since his teens. Dawlish had known other men who had been dedicated to their job in the police and who had never married. Married life, as such, was often a problem for a police officer who had to be away from home so much.

He put these thoughts out of his mind when Camilla Felista looked up. Again, her eyes were brimming and her lips were a little uneasy.

'Mr. Deputy,' she said. 'I have the permission to come with you.'

'Wonderful!' Dawlish enthused. 'Can you be ready by...'

She still would not let him finish a sentence; that habit of interrupting was going to annoy him one day, and might annoy others still more. But at the moment she was tremendously excited, and it was not fair to judge her except on performance.

'I have the mother,' she announced. 'I have asked her to prepare for me. My luggage will be at the airport. What, please, can I more do for you?'

'You can send these'—Dawlish touched the documents she had prepared—'to London, and also copies to...' He named half a dozen police forces, including New York and Los Angeles, Paris and Tokyo.

'Sir,' she said.

'Yes?'

'Why not to all the forces of police?'

'Can it be done?'

'To all from whom you have messages and who are named, yes of course. The colonel has instructed me to give all possible help. I tell you,' she went on, and so vital was her expression, so expressive her lips and eyes, that for the first time he forgot how homely she was; in fact, how ugly. 'I tell you, the colonel is a man of intelligence and integrity. He does not talk so much to strangers, he is a shy man. But he talks to me. Often he has talked of the Crime Haters. Twice, he was a delegate, but you will not remember. He considers that the Crime Haters organisation will become the best for the world. It will be the organisation which makes crime much more difficult and so much less. If the big criminals are not successful, he says, the small criminals will be discouraged.' She caught her breath and then flashed a question: 'You agree, yes?'

'I think I agree,' answered Dawlish.

'Good! To the colonel you are a great man. When he heard last night you were to come he was without sleep. He himself came to me and said "Camilla, quick," in the middle of the night, "there is work to do. We have the chance to help the Englishman, Dawlish, and his friends. With both hands we must seize it." So, we worked together, to be ready for you.' She paused, and then flashed another question, hardly giving herself time to catch her breath. 'When there is the attack on Miss Lee he is very distressed. But I myself heard him order Lieutenant Alfonso: "If the senhorita is in danger, with your life you protect her." And,' went on Camilla fiercely, 'it was so.'

'He was as brave as a man can be,' Dawlish said.

'Yes. Now, the colonel is glad I am to come to help. It is for him the cause, you understand.'

'For you, Camilla,' Dawlish said. 'What is it for you?'

'For me?' she echoed, taken aback for the first time. 'What is it for me?' She gave a sudden, enormous grin. 'For me, it is the *job*. I travel. I use all my languages where they began—I speak seven languages nearly perfect. The colonel—he is the idealist. I, Camilla Felista. I am the realist! *Now!* I send these summaries of the reports. And I tell you, a car waits to take you to the place where Miss Lee is resting and where you will find food waiting for you. On the aircraft, I see you.'

She went to the door and opened it wide for them.

In the heat of the day the beauty of the island seemed of less importance than the bodily discomfort. But when they stepped off the beach road into the club it was beautifully cool. Punkahs swayed to and fro, creating a breeze in addition to the air-conditioning. There were low-lying bamboo chairs and post-chaises, reed carpets of a dark beige colour, colourful murals and porcelains. And in a small room, alone, Catherine was reading some American magazines. She had a bandage round her head, covered by a silk scarf in the attractive style of a North American Indian.

'Don't get up,' Dawlish said. 'How are you?'

'Except for a headache,' she answered, 'I'm fine. I'm nearly over the shock, too.'

She put her face up, for Gordon Scott; and, obviously without thinking, he kissed her cheek. Then a small man in a pale blue waisted jacket and pyjama-type trousers came for their drink orders, recommending rum and lemon with sugar. When it came it was ice cold and delicious. Another steward brought sandwiches, fruit, bread, butter and honey; a third, coffee.

The meal lasted an hour and a quarter.

It was like balm, Dawlish thought. And he watched the young people and was astonished at their complete oblivion to everything and everyone else.

It was like a honeymoon.

But at last they were taken to the airfield, subjected to a few more minutes of that roasting heat, then into the big jet airliner which they were to share with a dozen other passengers who would land at Lagos.

Nothing had been discovered at the University Convalescent Home except some copies of the University of Salvador *Student Action*. On the front was the picture with its caption: '*Brutes*'.

The colonel, with at least six of his entourage, stood in the dazzling sunlight to see Dawlish's party off and stayed there until the great dark streaks from the jets had merged with the atmosphere and the aircraft could be no more than a dot in the sky.

Among the police chiefs who received Camilla's summary was Randy Patton.

He had received official approval for his forthcoming trip, and was busy clearing up local affairs. Although he never allowed his work to accumulate, a sudden departure at short notice invariably necessitated a mountain of instructions to be prepared for subordinates.

When he read the reports, he whistled.

'Pat must have got a computer for himself,' he remarked: and he repeated the jest to Dodie when, later that evening, he telephoned her at the apartment of a friend. He was chuckling as he said it, and then added almost in comic surprise: 'It couldn't be your Gordon, could it?'

'I doubt it,' Dodie said in a tone of voice which made him say:

'What's the trouble, honey? Is something bothering you?'

'I haven't heard from Gordon for three days,' she said.

111

'Is that for *ever*?'

'It's a long time for him,' she said. 'He called me every night when he first arrived. Daddy...'

'Yes, honey?'

'He's okay, isn't he?'

'I've had this summary from Pat Dawlish, and he would have said if there was any trouble,' Patton answered. 'Hon, you know what a policeman's life is like. There might be weeks when he can't get in touch with you. Don't let it upset you.'

But it did upset her. As she walked away from the building, she was oblivious of the deep blue of the sky and the mass of the Rocky Mountains carved out of the blue. She could think of nothing but Gordon. She told herself that it was madness, and unreasonable, and unfair, but it still worried her. If Gordon had thought it unlikely that he could telephone or write, he would have warned her. This was so unlike him. It was almost as if, having seen her again after a lapse of many months, he did not feel the same as he had in London.

CHAPTER FIFTEEN

GOLANA

Dawlish stretched himself as far as he could in the reclining chair, and looked out of the small window. Part of his view was obscured by the huge wing, and he could see the flames of the engine firing as it propelled them at nearly 700 miles an hour through the azure sky. Over to the south was a range of mountains, and the sun glinted on the snow on the topmost peaks. Below them and on either side was open country. Here and there the leaf-tipped branches of fever trees were vivid yellow in the evening sunlight. Here and there, too, was a huge baobab tree, its trunk swollen and shapeless, its branches thin and spidery like new life from a tree cut down savagely to the trunk. But for the most part of it was undulating country with a covering of pale brown grass waving gently in a wind which hardly stirred the trees. A pool reflected the sky like a mirror, rising from some underground spring; the animals were already gathering. Baboons and deer and wildebeest, giraffe and wild hog, at one a cluster of buffaloes, their great thick shoulders bent. At a big hole fringed by felled trees was a herd of elephants, gambolling, filling their trunks, squirting water muddy from their own trampling. Everyone in the aircraft went towards the windows to see this, and the radio suddenly crackled.

'On the right there is a herd of elephants, at least twenty strong—several families together. They've obviously taken over the pool. If you follow the path they made through the trees you will see they were at another pool last night. They knocked the trees down as they moved camp for the night.' There was a pause before the speaker went on: 'They eat the leaves off the lower branches of a tree and if they want more, they push the tree over and eat from the top when it's on the ground. Cunning creatures, elephants.'

There was a general titter of laughter.

'Further to the left are the Astiol Mountains,' the pilot went on. 'We are now about fifty minutes' flying time from Gola airfield, and we shall arrive at six-twenty precisely. We've already had clearance from airport control. If there's any change in the timetable I'll keep you informed, but I don't anticipate any. Thank you, everybody.'

He switched off.

Dawlish straightened his chair. Just in front, heads close together, sat Gordon Scott and Catherine, relaxing. There hadn't been much time to relax until now. Dawlish had been through every report and Gordon Scott and Catherine had checked the summary which Camilla had made. Camilla, occupying another row of seats, had begun a list of delegates who had accepted the suggestion of Gola as the rendezvous, and from time to time went to the pilot's cabin to have radio messages sent out to delegates. She came from the cabin as Dawlish straightened up, and gave him a wide smile.

'There is the question of wives,' she said, flatly.

'We can't invite them here,' said Dawlish.

'It is the wish of the President of Golana that those wives who wish to come should be the guests of the state,' said Camilla. 'I have just discussed this situation with him. I suggest, sir, the permission to request your office in London to send out the invitations.' She was obviously very set on rights for women.

'I'll think about it,' he promised.

For a moment he thought she was going to try to force the issue there and then; instead she gave way gracefully, and settling back in her seat, crossed her legs and then her wrists. She closed her eyes. A moment or two later Dawlish looked across again, and she seemed to be asleep. That wasn't surprising, for she must have been working at tremendous pressure for nearly twenty-four hours.

He pondered the wisdom of having women at the conference.

It had been done in London the previous year, and proved to be highly successful. But then there had been months of warning, and London was a woman's Mecca. Out here, what would they find to do? Half a day would be enough to cover the shops!

On the whole, he was against the proposal; but Felicity, his wife, seemed to be looking over his shoulder.

114

Soon they began to lose height from the 30,000 feet at which they had been cruising. There were signs of people below. Here and there were crescent clusters of round huts, with some kind of thatch for the roofs. They were all to the same pattern: a crescent of about twenty huts, a smaller one of five, and a much larger, central building. There were children, playing; and what seemed to be older children sitting as if at an outdoor school—yes! There were benches, and a teacher at a blackboard. Soon, the city itself began to show up, and for the first time the River Gola, which gave the country and the city its life, showed flat and bright against the brownish earth. Along the banks the trees and undergrowth were vivid green; it seemed to give the vegetation life, too. At some bends were great mud-flats, and everywhere the river was wide.

Dawlish had seen aerial pictures of the city but had not realised how new it was, nor its symmetry. It was obviously based on the Washington plan of great boulevards running round the heart of the city, streets spreading out from the centre; it was like a huge, white, spider's web.

Someone at the front said in tones of astonishment: 'Why, it's beautiful!'

And from here it was.

There was a big, domed central building, the very heart of the city. Then, ring after ring of shopping thoroughfares, built like those in New Delhi, with a covered walk. In the centre there seemed no cars except those which went along roads which bisected each other, to form a cross within a circle. Dawlish closed his eyes for a moment, but the picture was engraved on his mind like the sun's image after one had looked momentarily into it.

And around the outer circle were flags, fluttering gently; *hundreds* of flags, of all nations.

It was as if Golana was ready to receive not simply a police convention, but a gathering of the United Nations.

The radio crackled; and the *'no-smoking, fasten seatbelts'* sign was switched on.

'We're about to land, ladies and gentlemen. The roar as we touch the runway is quite normal as we brake and go into reverse to lower speed. We shall be fifteen minutes on the runway while the health people come out and spray the aircraft with insecticides. Malaria and yellow fever are no joke out here! But the Golana authorities have it thoroughly under control.'

They touched down; the engine roared; trucks came up manned by the Negro Golanans in a yellowish khaki uniform of waisted and belted bush jackets, shorts with a flare just above the knee, and sandals. They all wore berets of the same yellow colour. Great streams of water and what seemed like white steam covered the fuselage and the windows; for a few minutes it was as if they were being shut off from the world. Then the windows dried, and the aircraft taxied towards the single-storey airport building. As the doors were opened and the steps lowered, three men came from the building. It was all very like Vadife. The passengers alighted, Dawlish's group being the last to leave. The trio were at the foot of the steps, and Dawlish recognised the one in the middle who, like Junta, had been at the London conference.

Dawlish gripped his hand.

'Captain M'gobo—good to see you again.'

The other's eyes lit up. He was tall and ebony-faced, with a very smooth skin.

'And good to see you. Deputy Assistant Commissioner.' They gripped hands. 'Please meet Lieutenant Daho, who will be seconded to you for the convention building and the conference.' Daho was nearly as tall as M'gobo, a bigger, heavier man. His hand grip almost crushed Dawlish's unprepared fingers. 'And Lieutenant Hehi who will provide assistance and guides for the town.'

They were obviously glad to see Dawlish; to welcome the others; to guide them quickly through customs. It was warm but not unbearably hot, either inside or out.

'It was thought that you would be tired after your journey,' Captain M'gobo said. 'So no formal arrangements have been made for tonight, which you will spend at leisure. At half-past nine tomorrow morning you will be officially received by the President, and afterwards visit the university and the campus. It is beautiful,' he went on, with a kind of sigh in his voice. 'Beautiful. And our young people are so eager to learn. It is not good to think that here, also, there could be disturbances.'

'Before it's open?' Dawlish asked incredulously.

'There is a rumour that some of the registered students are being incited to demand that there be no European or American professors or lecturers, and half of the faculty is white,'

116

said M'gobo. 'So if you can find a way of quelling the disturbances at the other universities you could be doing us a very great service also. But enough of business, for tonight.'

It was tempting to say: 'We should work.' But Camilla looked to be asleep on her feet, Catherine was obviously tired. Dawlish said nothing. They were taken in a closed car to the centre circle, and one segment had a black sign, saying: *Capitol Hotel*. Barefooted Golanans came softly; there was an air of efficiency everywhere, the hotel foyer was large and cool, the open staircase of a handsome red wood. Each bedroom had a patio overlooking the Capitol building—comprising, M'gobo told them, the Government House, Parliament and most of the government offices. The walls were of off-white plaster with some animal murals in sepia; everything was cool and comfortable. Food, at a table in a large dining-room on the first floor, was simple but good—melon, chicken, fruit salad. The service was pleasant and unobtrusive.

Camilla, drinking coffee, said: 'I would like, please, to go to bed early.'

'All of us will,' said Dawlish.

'And in the morning . . .'

'We shall be given a VIP tour and then shown the university and where we shall work,' Dawlish told them. 'Good night, Camilla, Gordon, will you take Camilla up to her room?'

'Of course!' Gordon jumped up.

For the first time since they had met, Dawlish was alone with Catherine. She watched the others disappear, and then turned to look at him evenly. There was a soft murmur of music, just outside. He wondered what was going through her mind; wondered also why she so appealed to Gordon Scott. It was probably the kind of glow which radiated from her eyes, even from her skin; as if she were touched with some inner fire. Was that fanciful?

He felt his own heart beating fast.

'It's hard to believe there could be trouble here,' she said at last.

'No harder than to believe that you were nearly murdered in Vadife,' he replied.

'Do you think there is really danger in Gola?'

'Yes,' Dawlish answered.

'Thank you for being frank, anyway.'

'Isn't that what you would prefer?'

117

'In a way,' she answered. 'But sometimes ignorance *can* be bliss.' Her smile seemed free enough despite her words. 'It's all happened so quickly it's hard for me to grasp it. Will you answer me one question?'

'If the answer isn't an official secret!'

'Do you *really* think there is a single cause of the student revolts?'

Dawlish hesitated, and then answered quietly: 'There is a certain amount of dissatisfaction and discontent, some justified, some borne out of prejudice, to be expected. And whatever we manage to do there will always be trouble of a kind. But there's a savagery about this particular revolt, a violence, a passion which I feel sure is caused by a single group or organisation. If we can find out who, or what, that is then I think each university will be able to cope with its own problems.'

'Do you know who it is?' asked Catherine, and suddenly laughed. 'If you did, the answer *would* be an official secret, wouldn't it? Let me ask another question. Do you think the convention here will solve anything?'

'It could go a long way to finding out what we want to know,' Dawlish said. 'I . . .'

He broke off in sudden alarm, for Scott came striding from the foyer. At the same moment the quiet of the building and the Capitol centre was broken by the wailing of a siren which conveyed a note of stinging urgency. Other diners looked at Scott, startled. The waiters stood and stared out of the doorway towards the foyer, still silent, but obviously touched with alarm.

Scott reached the table.

'There's a big fire,' he said flatly. 'I'm told it's at the university.'

The roaring of an engine and the wailing of more sirens almost drowned his last words. Dawlish gripped Catherine's arm as they left the table for the front of the hotel. They reached it as Lieutenant Hehi, moving with beautiful rhythm, came in from the street.

'Mr. Dawlish,' he said, 'we wish to make sure you have all the protection needed. We have men outside the hotel, back and front. Also, we have guards at the corridors leading to your rooms, and outside each room. For your own protection, please, come upstairs.'

Obviously this was as much an order as a request.

118

They passed at least ten policemen, all looking immaculate, all armed, on the way to their bedrooms, which were off the same landing. Dawlish wondered what Scott and Catherine would do: talk in one room or another, or go into their separate rooms.

He decided for them.

'Gordon, until everything's clear, I want you to stay with Catherine.' As he spoke one of the hotel servants opened a door and they went through. As the door closed, two policemen stood at ease, outside it. Camilla's door was closed; he wondered whether she had gone off into a heavy sleep, or whether the noise of the alarms had disturbed her. He put the thought out of his mind as he turned to Hehi.

'Where is Captain M'gobo?'

'At the university, sir.'

'Take me there, please,' Dawlish said.

'Mr. Deputy Assistant Commissioner, my instructions are . . .'

'To take me to Captain M'gobo,' Dawlish said sharply.

For a moment he thought the little man would defy him, but at the last moment Hehi turned smartly, and hurried downstairs. There was an atmosphere of alarm, well concealed and yet unmistakable. It showed in eyes and the set of lips, the way people looked at each other.

The way they looked at *him*, Dawlish.

At first, he had not been aware of it, but now he was acutely conscious that the police, the hotel staff, the people just outside, looked at him in stark hostility. And as he stepped towards a car, a stone passed close by his head and clanged on the roof; almost at once another struck a pillar of the verandah only inches from his head. He stooped down to get into the car, and the moment he did so the opposite door opened and a face appeared.

It was dark-skinned. The man had very bright eyes and an open mouth and glistening white teeth. The rest of the body was in darkness of the shadow thrown by the car, but there was no shadow over the knife in his hand. It gleamed uncannily, the hand almost invisible, but the steel of the knife glistened like silver.

Death was only an instant away.

Instead of backing; or stopping; or heaving himself to one side, Dawlish flung himself forward. He felt a sharp pain at the side of his head, then the impact as his body struck the other man—on head or face or chest, he did not know. But he heard the gasp of breath, and a clattering sound, heard first shouting, then a shot. He fell. He was lodged between the backs of the front seats and the front of the back, which was a bench type. Light suddenly shone, vividly bright.

'Is he all right?' That was Hehi, and desperation sounded in his voice.

'I do not know, Lieutenant.'

Dawlish raised his head. He was dazzled by a torch which was immediately switched off. He heaved himself up until he could twist his body round and sit on the bench seat. More lights appeared. In the glow he saw a man stretched out on the road, another kneeling over him; there was a tiny rivulet of blood running down the first man's cheek.

Hehi was behind him, calling in anguish:

'Deputy Assistant Commissioner, are you all right? Please answer, are you hurt?'

'I'm fine,' said Dawlish. 'Not hurt at all.'

'But your head! It is bleeding!'

'It's a scratch,' Dawlish said, taking out a handkerchief. 'I want to get out to the university at once.' He leaned forward and gripped the lieutenant's shoulder. 'It will be all right, don't worry.'

'If you had been killed I would have killed myself,' stated Hehi in a quivering voice. They started at each other intently, until suddenly the Golanan said: 'Very well. Let us go.'

He climbed in with Dawlish and gave instructions to a man who took the wheel. Soon they were travelling fast along the highway which bisected the city. There were people on either side; hundreds of people, walking; *thousands* walking, hundreds cycling towards a glow which shone brighter and brighter against the star-strewn eastern sky.

CHAPTER SIXTEEN

PHOENIX

The police car passed the leaders of the surging crowd, and then a lighted sign reading *To Airport*. The fire was still miles away but now it appeared to spread across the whole horizon. The tall bush grass, the occasional trees, stood against the dull red background, from which tongues of flame leapt and died, leapt and died. Soon it was possible to see a line of cars against the flames. Men moved about, dark, cartoon-animated figures. Dawlish was now so near that he could see the sparks flying, and jets of water curving in great arcs which splayed out and became sparkling red.

A policeman on traffic duty, standing beneath a frond awning on a wooden platform, flashed a torch. The driver pulled up. Another policeman came from the side and peered in; then his heels clicked.

'Lieutenant.'

'Where is Captain M'gobo?'

'At the south gate, Lieutenant.' The man stood back, saluting again.

Now the men in the car could see the outlines of the buildings, the uprights and the cross struts and the roof girders. One after another these crashed down. They must surely be made of wood, Dawlish thought. The whole of the building was ringed with men, and he could see the water, from hydrants or springs nearby, was playing on the ground around the main buildings which were not on fire. There must be a thousand men within sight, working unceasingly. The scene gave an impression of efficiency which both surprised and impressed Dawlish.

Then the car drew up at a gateway where men were standing by several other vehicles. Dawlish opened the door and got out. Hehi came running round after him as M'gobo, face a dusky red in the glow, came striding across.

'Captain M'gobo, I can't tell you how sorry I am about this,' Dawlish said.

'You are not so sorry as the perpetrators will be when they are caught,' M'gobo scowled, anger roughening in his voice.

'Do you know who they are?' asked Dawlish.

'We know they are students,' M'gobo answered icily. 'We shall find them. Can you guess why they started this fire?'

'To make it impossible to hold the police convention,' Dawlish replied. He had no doubt about that at all, and could understand the anger the people felt for him. He had begun this convention, he was in one way to blame for the disaster.

'That is the truth,' M'gobo said. 'Now I can tell you that when it was announced that the Crime Haters were to come here, the President immediately received threats: he was ordered to cancel the convention or have the university destroyed. And later, today, there was a secret radio transmission telling the people you would bring bad luck and perhaps pestilence and famine to Golana. Some of our people are very superstitious. One such attempted to kill you tonight. He was a fanatic, but...' M'gobo shrugged and made the reflected flames dance on the metal of his shoulder flashes and the peak of his cap. 'It is a matter of time before the superstitions die.'

Dawlish said: 'Yes.'

He was looking at the flames demolishing the building which meant so much to the new country, and was thinking again: I really caused this. If he had not suggested Golana, then there would have been no fire, no fears, no losses.

'Mr. Dawlish,' began M'gobo, and then stopped; and gasped as if in anguish. A stab of flame broke the blackness of the buildings which had not been afire. Another and another flame stabbed. 'Look there!' he cried, speaking in his native tongue, swift and musical although now drenched in dread. Men began to run. M'gobo and Hehi began to run also, towards the new outbreak of flames, snatching fire brooms as they passed the stand.

And Dawlish began to run.

He snatched a fire broom and headed for a corner where the flames seemed to be gaining a hold. He passed several hurrying men and reached the corner. The building was of wood frames, and the light was good enough for him to see that there were no walls, as such, but a kind of venetian blind. Some of these were catching alight. He smacked at them with his broom and knocked some off, but more were catching alight. A stream of flame was coming from a drum set in the middle of this huge room.

Liquid streamed out, catching fire as it neared the ground.

Dawlish thought, almost as a reflex action: if we could get that away . . .

Quick as the thought, he snatched off his jacket, went to the far side of the drum, and wrapped the jacket round it. Then, he put his great arms around the drum itself, and enfolded it. He could reach right round it. He felt the liquid pouring. He put his forefinger into the hole and plugged it. Something spilled cold about his hand, up his sleeve, around his wrist. He turned. Fire was all about him but there was one stretch which had not caught. Steadily, he stepped towards it. He felt the heat of flames at his back. He knew that the inflammable liquid on his clothes and body was giving off fumes which might burst into flames at any moment; a single explosion would engulf him. He gritted his teeth and half-closed his eyes, but was still able to see the gap.

Blinds were down, he would have to grope his way through them. His heart dropped, and for the first time he felt a wave of hopelessness and with that, a surge of fear. His heart leapt widly and he began to breathe very fast. For the first time, too, he began to quicken his pace. He could feel the contents of the drum lapping up and down. He kicked against a ridge in the ground and nearly stumbled. He was gasping for breath, and his lips, his gums, his mouth and tongue seemed afire.

The blinds moved.

Men beyond them were pulling them away. Others were making a tunnel of torchlight, shining it downwards so that he could see the path. He stepped over the low wall of the opening from which the blind had been taken, reached the other side safely, then began to walk.

'Long strides,' he muttered aloud.

'Don't jolt it.'

'Long strides.'

He saw flame, just above him; *above* him. My God, his back was alight. His hair! He felt his body hunch and his heart lurch. Then he felt something cool on his back: cool and stinking. Someone had closed on him from behind and was using a fire extinguisher. A miracle! He saw a little circle of light a few yards ahead. Several men were shining their torches down towards the same spot. Why should they do that? Why? *Ah!* He could put the drum down there. Careful, careful, put it down. But it was so heavy and his whole body was pain-racked. He couldn't bend. He simply could not bend.

Two men came to him. Neither spoke, but each stretched out his arms in front of him and linked hands, making a 'chair'. Why—*ah!* Blind fool! He slowed down and stopped. They waited until he reached them and lowered the drum; his arms felt like breaking, but at last the weight was no longer on his arms but on theirs.

They carried it away.

The flames leapt and roared and the whole night was one lurid glare but in the glare were shapes. Faces. Dark faces, bright eyes, bright lips. Faces. Mouths wide open. White teeth showing. What were they going to do? *Eat him?* Bloody fool. There was a new kind of noise. A chanting. Chanting. Cheering! My God, they were cheering him.

Then he was surrounded. He saw M'gobo but not Hehi. He felt men supporting him. He was led to a car—no, a Land Rover. He was helped in. In most places where they touched him, he hurt. He felt brittle. He wanted a drink. He was parched. There was movement in front of his face; and they were offering him water.

M'gobo appeared.

'The fire is dying out,' he stated quietly. 'The main building was not destroyed.' He added something which sounded like 'Thanks to you.' The engine started. There were chanting, cheering people and roaring engine. The headlights showed two rows of people, forming a path. Policemen were pushing them back. Beyond the first rows there was movement. He could see from this height, the crowd was running behind the front lines to catch another glimpse of him. Cheering, chanting, running, roaring . . .

Soon, he was at a hospital. Dark-faced doctors, dark-faced nurses, touched and tended him. What salve they used he did not know, but it brought immediate soothing. Here and there they applied a plaster, here and there a bandage. They gave him another drink, of what he knew not, and it eased his aching head and his burning eyes. Then a nurse, dark and pretty, held up a burned rag, in front of his eyes.

'Your coat,' she said, and laughed; and others laughed. And for a moment he was nonplussed, but suddenly he knew just what to say.

'If my coat's like that, what are my trousers like?'

He had never heard such laughter or seen such radiance on human faces.

When he got back, Catherine and Gordon Scott were waiting in the lounge, eager to see him. Word had spread fast. Every man and woman in the hotel was smiling. Only Camilla seemed to have slept through the excitement. Even Catherine seemed excited.

'I think this is the first time I've realised what a hero you are,' she said.

'Oh, nonsense!' exclaimed Dawlish.

'If that's nonsense, I'm a student rabble-rouser,' Scott declared.

When Dawlish went to bed a few tender spots manifested themselves, but none bad enough to keep him awake. His last thoughts were of what the police would do to find the fire-raisers and the secret radio transmitter. There could be savage vengeance; he hoped against hope that this would not be so.

During the night, the police and the army were out in force.

One after another, suspects were caught and brought in. Just before dawn, a man-made cave near the banks of the Gola River was discovered, with the transmitting station and two men in it—dead of knife wounds.

It was nearly eight o'clock when Dawlish woke, to find a tea-tray by his side, and a copy of the *Golana Drum*. The front page was given over to the fire and to Dawlish; a whole inside page was given to the coming conference of policemen. If there had been the slightest doubt before, there was none now: Golana was proud of being host to the world's police.

At nine o'clock, a car flying the President's flag on the bonnet was drawn up outside the hotel, waiting, and a crowd at least three thousand strong burst into cheers when Dawlish appeared. He stood for a moment, one hand raised, and thus had time to see how spacious and attractive were the walks, the colonnades, the steps leading up to the Capitol building. It was warm but not over hot. The sun was bright and every building looked as if it had been painted only that morning. The streets were immaculate, the windows were well dressed and the people seemed as happy as they were excited.

Soon, the party was on its way to the President's palace on

the other side of the Capitol circle, the home of the third President of Golana. As Dawlish and the others appeared at the foot of a long flight of snow-white steps, President N'lawi appeared at the front doors of the palace. He was a short, very square-shouldered man, wearing a pale grey lounge suit with no decorations. Above him the flags of Britain and Golana fluttered, and the flags of all nations were stirred about the perimeter of the great circle.

Dawlish stepped forward.

'Mr. Dawlish,' said N'lawi, in a deep, pleasing voice. 'You are very welcome, as your friends are and will be. I want you please to understand that we of Golana will forever be grateful to you, personally.'

Dawlish said: 'I only wish I could have done more.'

'Had you not done what you did, the whole of the main university complex would have been destroyed,' went on N'lawi. 'As it is, the damage was confined to sleeping quarters for the delegates. Happily, no furniture was inside. The building will be rebuilt in good time, the fire will have delayed nothing.' He turned to the others. 'You are equally welcome,' he said, and then led them inside the palace.

There was no pomp or ceremony but there was a feeling of great sincerity in all that followed.

'We shall place all the facilities of Golana at your service,' said the President. 'For this is a way of revealing ourselves to the whole world. What we seek here, Mr. Dawlish, is a model society.' There was a glint in his eyes when he went on: 'Indeed, a crime-free society.'

'I'll do what I can to help you achieve it,' Dawlish said earnestly.

He had never meant anything more.

Dawlish said to M'gobo, after the official welcome:

'He can't be serious: those buildings can't be rebuilt in four days.'

'They can be and they will be,' M'gobo assured him. He laughed. 'They were wooden frames with frond roofing and blinds which could be lowered to make walls against the wind or the rain. It is not such a miracle. Now, Mr. Dawlish! I wish to take you and your colleagues to the Police Operations Room. Here, because of limited resources, it combines with our internal and overseas radio and teletype links. What we

126

have is small, but most up-to-date. I believe that Miss Felista will be very pleased!'

Camilla was delighted.

Here was a control-room with everything needed by a modern police force. Here were instantaneous links with the whole world. Along one side of the Communications Room electricians—one out of six or seven a European—were working on an electronics system for contact with the rest of the world's police forces.

'Mr. Dawlish,' cried Camilla, 'it is the super marvellous!' And her eyes glistened as she began to examine the machines and all the facilities. 'Is it so that Miss Lee will be here to assist me?'

'Yes.'

'I ask nothing more—except of course your help,' she flashed at M'gobo.

'You will have all you need,' M'gobo replied. 'Now, Mr. Dawlish! If you and Inspector Scott will come with me.' He led the way to an underground room, where there were a dozen cells, as familiar to Dawlish as those at Scotland Yard. In each cell, two young men sat, glum and even despairing.

'These men are suspected of helping to start the fires,' M'gobo said simply. 'They are awaiting trial and if found guilty they will be sentenced to death. However, they all say the same thing: they were paid to start the fires by two students, both Golanans, who operated a radio transmitter.

'These two young men were found murdered, and their transmitter smashed,' went on M'gobo. 'You are still far from your objective, Mr. Dawlish.'

Dawlish said gruffly: 'Yes. Whatever you do, keep Miss Lee safe.'

'No harm shall come to her,' M'gobo assured him earnestly. 'She is a friend of yours and for a long time you will be the most popular man in Golana.'

No doubt he meant it.

As he had meant what he said about the university.

Dawlish was at the airport, about to take off, when Camilla came running from an official car, a piece of paper in her hand. As she drew nearer she called: 'A cable, please, from Commissioner Patton.' She thrust the cable into Dawlish's hand, and he looked down and read:

'One hundred and seven university campus editions of *Stu-*

dent Action in this country have identical articles, pictures and captions except for local campus news which is mostly disruptive and revolutionary.'

'That's exactly what I hoped for,' Dawlish said, and tucked the cable into his pocket.

As he flew off towards London, his last glimpse was of men swarming about the burned-out site, taking away charred rubble on huge litters made, as far as he could judge, of sticks bound together by leather thongs. Others were bringing up big timbers. A small circular saw was whirling, whirling.

The accommodation would be ready for the delegates, beyond doubt.

But what could the delegates do when they got here? Were they any nearer at all to the murderous killer-force which had lined up behind the students?

Why *was* Catherine so important to those who directed it?

Why *had* they tried to prevent the Crime Haters from meeting here?

What profit could be gained out of the student rebellions? And what was the overall plan?

In every waking minute, Dawlish concentrated on these questions. The answers must exist and the police must find them. He did not get out of the aircraft but contemplated the uniform type of airport building and the distant outline of the city. Five new passengers boarded, and he watched them with great concentration until he made sure none was student young. He almost laughed at his own tension. Then, fifteen minutes after take-off, when he went along to the washroom, he saw the headlines of a newspaper which lay on a seat next to one of the newcomers. It read:

STUDENT PROTESTS AGAINST WORLD POLICE
CONFERENCE

He stood stock still, reading, oblivious of everything else, even of the passenger who had brought the newspaper on board and was now staring at him.

128

CHAPTER SEVENTEEN

STUDENT ACTION

The first paragraph in the article, in bold type, read:

'Students throughout the world are up-in-arms against the international police conference to be held next week in Golana, to discuss worldwide student rebellions. Police headquarters in many major cities have been surrounded by angry student-rebels, many armed. They carry banners and posters, saying: "We are students, not criminals." "Cops, fight crime, not students." "Call the anti-learning conference off." '

There were many other quotations, but Dawlish did not read them all. He went on and tapped at the door of the cockpit. A stewardess opened it, and let him in. Just ahead was the mass of controls on the panels, the pilot in one seat, co-pilot in another. The radio officer sat at a tiny alcove, earphones over a bald head; apart from his baldness, he looked very young.

'How can we help you?' asked the co-pilot.

'Do you think I could speak to my office?'

'Yes, Sparks will fix that for you.'

Obviously the radio officer was tuned in to the co-pilot, for he nodded at once, and made room by his side.

'Bit noisy today,' he remarked. 'But you should be able to hear. Won't be long, sir.'

In fact, it was less than two minutes before he was speaking to Sills, whose voice was clear enough even though it faded now and again. Headphones kept out all sound from the engines, and up here Dawlish seemed remote from the world; he found it hard to realise that Sills had only to lift his eyes to look out on London and the Thames.

'Very glad to hear you, sir,' he said. 'We're having a hell of a lot of trouble.'

'Scotland *Yard*?'

'Absolutely besieged, sir—swarming round the place.' There was a chuckle in Sills' voice. 'Funny thing is, they don't

129

realise that our branch operates from the old building. Peaceful as a desert island here.'

Dawlish found himself chuckling.

'Nice work! I want a complete list of police headquarters having trouble, and . . .'

'That's being prepared, sir,' Sills said, with almost Camilla-like impulsiveness.

'I also want a list of each university which has a *Student Action* news-sheet or whatever they call it, published and sold on the campus—and I'd like specimens of them all. Ask each delegate to arrange it for next week, will you?'

'I suppose . . .' began Sills, and then broke off.

'You suppose what?'

'The conference *will* go on, sir. If they have any more trouble like they did at Gola last night there won't be anywhere to meet.'

'If it had to be held in the open air in Golana we could still stage it. What put that gloomy note in your mind?'

'Well, sir—oh, the blazes! Two or three M.P.s have taken the students' view. There's a lot of pressure being used to call the conference off. The *Daily Globe* runs a police-baiting editorial this morning: it says we've plenty of trouble in our own backyard, without going out of our way to create more trouble. I'm sorry to say it, but you're coming back to a hornets' nest. And . . .' Again he broke off, and seemed to swallow his words; and again Dawlish prompted him.

'Don't keep anything back,' he ordered.

'No, sir. I—ah—I wondered if it would be wise if you landed in Paris, say, or somewhere away from London Airport and slipped in on a B.E.A. plane or one of the European airways.'

'Well, well,' Dawlish breathed. 'They're preparing a reception party for me, are they?'

'I'm afraid so, sir.'

Dawlish laughed, but there was an edge to the sound, and he saw the radio-operator's eyebrows lift; the man could hear every word, in both directions, of course.

'Don't be afraid,' Dawlish said. 'Have plenty of men at the airport for crowd control, and have a public address outfit ready so that I can talk to the crowd from the steps of the aircraft.'

There was a long pause before Sills said uneasily:

'They're in a very excitable mood, sir. It would be easy to make trouble. I've good reason to believe that the Commissioner himself would be happier if you slipped into London quietly.'

That stopped Dawlish in his tracks.

Sills was fairly new. Dawlish's old assistant, Childs, would have gone on doing whatever Dawlish ordered, ready to shoulder all the responsibility. But Sills might be worried for his job; and might also think that it was wrong for Dawlish to come into head-on conflict with the students. One had to have known Dawlish for a long time before having absolute faith in him.

'Have you had any specific orders?' Dawlish asked.

'No, sir.'

'Then have that loud-speaker unit installed, but not on a police car,' Dawlish said.

'Major.' It was strange how many people dropped into the use of the old war-time title under pressure.

'Yes, Sills?'

'You *could* get a bullet in your head.'

'If I started to count the number of times I might have had a bullet in my head or in my belly, it would be like counting sheep.' Dawlish sounded angry; indeed he was angry. 'One other thing, Sills. Ask the C.I.D. to check on the *Daily Globe*, its attitudes and its politics, very closely, will you? Get out all its leaders and feature articles on the student situation. And find out which American and European associates or what subsidiaries it has.'

'My God!' exclaimed Sills.

'Get busy,' ordered Dawlish, and took the headphones off.

The radio officer took them from him and gave a broad, boyish grin.

'Now I believe everything I've ever heard of you,' he remarked. 'Very glad to be of help, sir. Count on me if there's any rough-stuff at the airport.'

The request for copies of the local *Student Action* went out at once, from London. Most police forces where there had been campus troubles already had them. Some were monthly journals but most were weekly. Copies from universities which had been quiet were also obtained. The American journals were sent, that day, to Patton in New York; and journals from

131

the universities in Europe were sent to the capital city police forces. They were collected in Australia, in Japan, in Russia; every country co-operated quickly.

And four detectives from Scotland Yard were detailed immediately to get information about the *Daily Globe*.

Gradually, a picture began to form for all the Crime Haters to see.

A picture which was not the result of deduction or detection, but simply of observation, formed in Dawlish's mind, as the aircraft circled in its slow descent to Heathrow. At first he saw only the highways with their miniature-seeming cars, the fields, the reservoirs, the little groups of houses which made the area look like a toy town. Then, looking down on the airport itself, he saw the masses of people.

They were jammed about the main airport building, on the top of the observation tower. They were marching along the highways—along the Great West Road and the roads from Staines, from Guildford, the south and east. They spewed into the airport off the M4 motorway; they were there in tens, perhaps in hundreds, of thousands.

They carried great banners.

They carried huge posters.

They had brass bands and pop groups, the sunlight glinting on their instruments.

They marched in military precision, and as he stared, Dawlish was quite sure of one thing. This was not a spontaneous outburst; it was a long-planned demonstration. It was orderly, far too orderly.

One of the other passengers touched Dawlish on the shoulder.

'Hate to sound a note of gloom,' he said, 'but aren't your chaps conspicuous by their absence?'

'They're dotted about,' Dawlish pointed out.

'You need brigades of troops, not a few scattered bobbies!'

'I don't doubt we can get them if we need them,' Dawlish said. He went along to the cockpit, where all the crew were gaping down. One of the stewardesses looked scared, the others almost excited.

'... they spread any further we won't be able to land.'

'Skipper,' Dawlish said. 'Will you tell ground control that I'll be off last?'

'Like a shot,' the beak-nosed captain said. 'I have expected to be diverted but they've given me all clear.'

'Good!' Dawlish said, as if he really meant it.

For a while they seemed to be crawling, but at last they touched down, bumped slightly and then roared along the runway. Over to the right, away from the airport buildings and control tower, masses of youths and girls were marching, banners and posters and flags waving. Around the airport itself there were the waiting thousands.

'They're so still,' the pilot remarked uneasily.

'Drilled to it,' put in Sparks.

Slowly, the aircraft taxied towards the buildings. Fire engines and ambulances were standing by. Steps were run up to the front and rear exits. Trucks rumbled to the luggage bays in the bowels of the aircraft. The passengers walked down the steps, the crew spoke to each in turn.

'Goodbye, sir.'

'Hope you enjoyed the trip, madam.'

'Glad to have had you with us, sir.'

At last, only Dawlish was left. He stood watching as a microphone was hauled up to the top of the steps. He noticed the few dozen policemen, standing quite calmly, and the massed ranks of the crowds. Now he could read the banners.

'Stop the cops!' cried one. 'Police hunt crooks, not students.' 'Ban the Police Conference.' 'We are students, not criminals.' 'Student Action' cried another boldly, and yet another: 'Student Power.'

Dawlish had to duck in order to get out of the cabin and on to the steps. A few policemen in their dark blue stood at the foot of the steps with airline officials. The stewards and stewardesses were gone, and so was the co-pilot, but the pilot was there, his nose almost quivering for action, and the radio officer, cap covering his baldness, was by his side.

Dawlish raised both hands—clasped and shook them above his head; and he gave the biggest grin he could, as if he thought this was the grand-daddy of all jokes. A moment's startled silence seemed profound, before a few among the crowd grinned back and one or two giggled.

Dawlish gave the boxer's salute again, and then, laughter in his voice, spoke into the microphone.

'This is the first time in my life,' he said in a voice made deep and resonant by the microphone, 'that I've ever had a

Beatles'-type reception.'

There was a gasp; then a positive roar of laughter. Before it died away, Dawlish went on:

'And I can't even sing!'

More laughter billowed out.

'I may not be a Beatle,' Dawlish boomed, 'and I may not know much about pop, but I *am* a good cop. How many of you know that I was in the secret service during the war, dropped, I forget how many times, behind the enemy lines? If I'd been seen I would have been shot or torn to pieces, but I was always lucky. The only time I was really in trouble was when there was a *very* clever Nazi commander in a Belgian village which was solidly pro-British. The commander was tipped off that English agents were being dropped, and he spread the rumour that we were Nazi parachutists in training. Then he let the villagers get at us. By the luck of the gods I knew one of the resistance workers and he saved our bacon. The Nazi was brilliant, of course. He wanted us killed by the resistance workers first, then he would have shot the resistance workers out of hand for having, and using, weapons. It was sheer bad luck that he didn't get what he wanted both ways.'

Dawlish paused, to draw a deep breath and spread his arms and say in a very different, icy voice:

'I'm *your* luck. But for me you would be caught between two fires. Do you know what I've got in my head?' He touched his head with his left hand, and went on: 'I've got absolute proof that you're all being taken for a ride. That people are using your justifiable grievances to get power. And by God, when they get it you'll be out of the frying pan into the fire. I...'

He heard a shout: 'Stop him!'

He turned towards it as hundreds of other heads turned.

He saw a man near the front of the crowd, with a gun levelled. He saw the face behind the gun. It was one of the two men whom Catherine had identified, suspected of killing Miraldi after helping to kick Gerald Lee to death. It was Kelly or Tyson, he wasn't sure which. Kelly—Tyson. Kelly—Tyson went through his mind as he flung himself to one side.

The crack of a shot was followed by another bellow from a different direction. A second crack, and metal smacked against the metal platform on which he was standing. Suddenly, police dived into the crowd, there was fierce struggling and thousands

134

surged back. Dawlish straightened up and took the micro-phone.

'Don't panic,' he called calmly. 'It's only a little struggle up front. And both bullets missed me. They didn't want that proof to get out, did they? But it will get out, all round the world. Just read your *Student Action*.'

Then he jumped down from the steps and walked, alone, towards the crowd.

A path opened for him.

CHAPTER EIGHTEEN

ACTION

Dawlish had an impression of young faces, male and female, of long hair and short hair; of smiles and of shouting, of surging and of swaying: but the surging was away from him. No police were needed to keep the crowd at bay. Once he was in the main lounge, however, his knees suddenly felt weak and first he stood very still and then he dropped into a chair. Someone offered him a flask but he shook his head; someone came hurrying with coffee, and he gulped it down.

Sills appeared, homely and chunky. And excited.

'Marvellous job, sir! Congratulations!'

'Good stuff, students,' Dawlish said. 'When they aren't being led by false prophets. Did you get the man?'

'He shot himself, sir, I'm afraid.' Glumness shadowed Sills's face but only for a moment. 'The other chap's alive.'

Dawlish's eyes brightened too. 'Tyson or Kelly?'

'Tyson, sir—fits the description to a T.'

'Now we shall be able to get a move on,' Dawlish said, with deep satisfaction. 'Have you started tracing their movements?'

'I called the Yard, sir. It's in hand. They were staying at one of those small hotels near the B.E.A. terminal, that much we have found out already. We can go whenever you like, sir. Customs and Immigration have cleared you.'

'Then let's go.'

'We've a motor-cycle escort, just in case there should be more trouble,' Sills explained. 'But that speech of yours was relayed all over the airport, sir—practically everyone heard it. I was watching from the control tower myself. Never seen such a change on people's faces. Quite restored my faith in human nature!'

'Don't let it fool you,' Dawlish said. 'When the crowd is young it's malleable, but when it gets past middle-age it's usually as stiff as a poker.'

He went with Sills and several other policemen in plain-clothes. Passengers for flights to all corners of the world stared; a few groups of youngsters, most of the men long-haired and wearing a wild assortment of jeans and jerkins, jackets and sweaters, furs and furbelows, gathered at various places; from two such groups there came a ragged cheer or two. A few stragglers were outside but obviously most of the crowd had been kept away from the actual building and near-approach roads. Out of sight, bands were playing. Three long-haired young people—sex undiscernible—walked up and down offering *Student Action* for sale much in the way that Salvation Army lassies offered *War Cry*. In its way, *Student Action* was another *War Cry*.

There were many more police about here.

'The tactics were to let them in and stop them from going out if there was trouble,' explained Sills. 'There were enough water hoses and foam inside the runway area to have sent the whole lot of baskets home with their tails between their legs. I will say again, sir, they were a much better-tempered bunch than I expected.'

'Ever been bad-tempered when everyone is gunning for you?' asked Dawlish. 'You had no problems, then.'

'No, sir. The Commissioner as well as the A.C. for Crime asked me what you'd said and I told them word for word. They approved right away, sir. And the A.C. Traffic was with them and he came out here and sorted things out with the Middlesex and airport police.' Sills was very pleased with himself indeed, but slowly his expression changed. He looked at Dawlish's head, and asked earnestly: '*Have* you got that proof of who's behind it, sir?'

Dawlish smiled faintly.

'I don't think a judge and jury would consider it proof.'

'But *you* do.'

'Proof enough to stake my life on. But we're not going to get it until we have an analysis of the contents and style of all the *Student Actions* round the world. What I need before I fly back to Gola is the report on the *Daily Globe* and its associates and subsidiaries.'

Sills said, smugly: 'You'll have it by the time you get back to the office, sir.'

'Good lord!' exclaimed Dawlish. 'To galvanise the offices into action I simply have to go away. Is that it?'

137

'Not quite, sir,' said Sills.

'What are you holding out on me?'

'Well, sir, if you don't mind my saying so, it's very easy for someone like you, in charge of the international aspect of the crime scene, to forget that the C.I.D. is at it all the time. You're involved only in crimes which might have overseas repercussions—I mean ramifications, sir. So a lot goes on you don't know about.'

'I am humbled,' Dawlish said, and sounded as if that were true indeed. 'Go on.'

'There's been some suspicions about Lord Elderwater, sir, who owns the Globe Newspapers, for some time. Some of the editorials are very nearly seditious. And there's always been doubt as to where he gets his money from. So the Yard's been quietly accumulating the facts about him, and his newspapers. Do you know, sir, there isn't a country in the world where he doesn't own or control a newspaper direct or through his subsidiaries?' Sills paused long enough for this to sink in, and added comfortably: 'It'll all be on your desk, and the team which prepared it is standing by.'

'Well, well,' exclaimed Dawlish. 'What it is to be one of a team! What we also need is a few editors who can study style . . .'

'There's a team at the Home Office working on that,' Sills informed him. 'And as soon as you asked for samples of *Student Action* we collected them from the British Museum—every university in Great Britain sends copies there. And we picked up some from a lot of embassies as well as from Commonwealth and Colonial government offices. Surprising how many we got in a couple of hours.'

'Sills,' said Dawlish, with feeling, 'I didn't know you could move so fast.'

'I know what you mean,' replied Sills, both glum and droll at the same time. 'That's been both a blessing and curse to me all my career—all my life, if it comes to that. I look so bloody slow—like a carthorse you might say, but I've only come across one man who could think and act faster.'

'Really? And who is this phenomenon?'

'You, sir,' Sills announced clearly.

Dawlish turned and stared full-faced into the man's eyes. The question must have sounded as if he were fishing, but the answer hadn't occurred to him. Taken aback on several

138

grounds, he seemed to be looking at Chief Superintendent George Sills for the first time: at a chunky face with a very wide jaw, a small, unexpectedly shapely mouth—almost feminine in its softness—rather heavy-lidded eyes, but the eyes themselves, honey-brown, were surprisingly clear. He had very silky hair, about the same colour as his eyes, and it was brushed so that a few streaks of his tanned cranium showed. He had a broad nose with wide nostrils: in fact, he looked a little like a bruiser dressed in his Sunday best.

'Sills,' said Dawlish, quietly, 'in future I am going to be much happier whenever I leave the office.'

'That's very reassuring,' said Sills. His eyes positively shone. 'Mind you, sir, I have blind spots. I can be a damned sight too impulsive for a policeman. Hope I haven't sounded as if I'm blowing my own trumpet too much.' When Dawlish didn't answer, he went on with new-found diffidence: 'The thing is, sir, since Childs retired and I took over we haven't had much of a chance to talk, or get to know each other.' And while Dawlish remained silent, he went on, quite gruffly: 'I've another bad fault, sir. I talk too much.'

'George,' said Dawlish at last, I think we're going to get along.' And without any preamble, he went on: 'Are you married?'

'Six years a widower, sir. Had a comfortable married life but I'm acclimatised to living on my own. My only daughter's married—lives in Canada.' And suddenly his eyes widened in consternation, and he almost cried: 'I forgot, sir. Your wife's back! She said could you possibly see her before you get down to work.

'Have me dropped at my place,' Dawlish decided, quickly. 'And work on the assumption that I'll be a couple of hours. And on call, of course.'

'Very good, sir,' said Sills.

A few minutes later, when the car pulled into the carriageway of one of the tallest buildings in London, on the Embankment close to Millbank, he sprang out and opened Dawlish's door—and his right hand hovered forward. Dawlish gripped it with a fervour as great as Sills's when he had gripped Dawlish's.

On that instant, Big Ben, which was just in sight, chimed four.

'Six o'clock, then,' Dawlish said, and hurried into the foyer and the lift which was already on the ground floor. He stepped out on to the landing on the penthouse floor, half-preoccupied with what Sills had told him and with the revelation of Sills, the man, half with the thought of seeing Felicity, his wife. One of the joys of his marriage was that there was excitement at the thought of meeting her when they had been separated even for a few days, as now.

The apartment door opened, and a man stepped out: a total stranger. From the passage behind Dawlish another man appeared, one whom Dawlish could hear but could not see.

'Don't shout, don't fight, just do as you're told,' ordered the man in the doorway. 'Come in and tell us exactly what secret you hold in your head. If you don't, if you lie, you'll never see your wife again.'

The shock was so great it was like being struck in the face with an iron bar. It swept through Dawlish, like pain. It actually rocked him back towards the lift, the doors of which were still open. It did flash through his mind that he could actually fall back into the lift, might manage to get the door closed, but as the thought came, whoever was behind him stepped between him and the lift and thrust him into the hall. He staggered again, unable to save himself; he could not stop, and actually went through into the flat and banged against the wall. Before he could regain his balance the two men pushed and shouldered him into the living-room; a magnificent room with panoramic windows along two sides, converging into a corner which had a sweeping view of the Houses of Parliament, of Lambeth Palace, Parliament Square, Whitehall and Trafalgar Square. On the distant skyline the slender spires of smaller churches stood like pencil strokes, dominated by St. Paul's; even the new, angular buildings seemed insignificant in comparison with it.

Dawlish had bought this penthouse because of the view.

Now, unsteady on his feet, he came up against a big couch, and dropped heavily into it. Then he was able to sit up squarely, facing the two men who stood in front of him. One held an automatic pistol; the other, a knife.

The smaller and slimmer of the two, the one with the gun, was fair-haired and good-looking in an unremarkable way, if one discounted very thin lips. The other was taller, dark-haired, with a bow-shaped mouth and a pointed nose and chin.

The smaller man was the spokesman.

'Now, what do you know?' he demanded, in a sharp voice.

Dawlish drew his hand across his forehead. He was trembling—partly with shock, partly with rage. His mouth was parched; even had he wanted to speak in those first moments, words would not have come.

When he didn't answer at once the spokesman rasped:

'You're not dealing with a bunch of kids now.'

'No,' Dawlish managed to croak. 'Do you know what I'd do now, if I acted on impulse?' His very manner made the men draw back, and tighten their grips on their weapons. 'I'd beat you both to pulp. So be thankful I haven't acted on impulse.'

'Dawlish, bluster won't help you.'

'Oh, don't be a bloody fool! Haven't you the sense to see that I'm trying to make up my mind what to do?' Neither of the others responded: his aggressiveness had shaken them. Slowly, grudgingly, he went on: 'While you've got my wife you think you've got the whip hand. Where is she?'

The man with the knife said: 'Stop wasting time.' He had a rather nasal voice, almost a whine.

'She's on the patio, tied hand and foot,' the other man said. 'No one can see her. This is the highest building for miles around. One push, and she would fall you-know-how-many feet to the concrete. *What do you know, Dawlish?*'

Dawlish moistened his lips.

'Right, then, here goes: Elderwater, the owner of the *Globe*, whose newspapers and magazines are distributed all over the world, is at the bottom of this. He finances pretty well all the editions of *Student Action* in every language under the sun, and he pays—this is a deduction from the rest—he pays teams of agitators to go round to the universities, find out what genuine grievances exist, find out which students are easy to influence, and works the campus into frenzy.'

He paused.

There was horror on the face of the smaller man, horror on the other man's. They were appalled, and in showing their reaction they were telling Dawlish how right he was. Not that there had been much doubt after Sills had talked about the inquiry into Elderwater's activities. When they turned back to him, he went on:

'Take over the universities and you take over the future. I don't know what your Lord High Chief wants—political con-

141

trol, economic control or just plain money.' When neither man spoke, he went on: 'I imagine the real cause is to set himself up as Lord Chief Dictator, while he cons the students into thinking it's an ideological one. God damn it!' he suddenly roared. 'You two ought to be old enough not to die for a megalomaniac who ...'

The man with the gun raised it.

'Shut up!'

'I'm not going to die,' the other man growled.

'Don't be a fool,' Dawlish said. 'You're as good as dead already.' He looked beyond them to the black, open doorway, and went on in the same voice: 'Aren't they, Sills?'

They started and turned their heads.

And as they turned Dawlish leapt at the one with the gun and struck him so savagely in the groin that the man squealed in agony, dropped the gun, and doubled up, his face already turning green. The other swung back, knife poised to throw. Dawlish simply leapt at him, felt the knife at his side, reached the man and picked him up and hurled him across the room. His body caught against the open door, and he fell in a strangely bent position.

Outside, on the patio, was Felicity.

Dawlish made himself dial 999, and talk to the Yard, before he put the receiver down and went out on to the patio. There was great dread in him, for they may have lied. Felicity might already be dead.

She was where the man had told him, her eyes wide open; he saw the enormous relief in them when he appeared. He did not quite know how he managed to smile, but he did. His fingers were steady as he unfastened the neckties used to tie her hands and feet, and to gag her. Then he began to tremble; and she began to mutter incoherently at first because her lips were so stiff and sore, but gradually she spoke more clearly.

'Oh, my darling,' she was saying. 'Oh, my darling, it's all right, don't worry, it's all right. Oh, Pat, my love, don't shiver so. *Please* don't shiver so.'

The police arrived, led by an appalled Sills, and took the prisoners away.

'We're doing very well at the office, sir,' Sills said to Dawlish. 'Why not wait until eight o'clock? Most of the reports will be ready then, sir. Oh, by the way: Lord Elderwater

142

killed himself when Special Branch men went to question him. You got at the truth streets ahead of us, now all we have to do is find the evidence you guessed was there.' He looked at Felicity in mock horror. 'What a job for a policeman!'

When he had gone, Felicity asked in a husky voice:

'Is it really all over, Pat? Can it be?'

She stood in the panoramic window, the sun's warmth and brightness reflected on her fair hair and complexion, on her clearly defined features which had for so long been beautiful to him. She was tall and very upright, in appearance wholly right as his partner. Now her anxiety showed in grey-green eyes which had the brightness of precious stones.

'No,' Dawlish said. 'It isn't all over, darling. There must be others—Elderwater couldn't have done all this on his own. We've cut off the head, as it were, but there's a lot of evil life left in the arms and legs. And everything that has happened shows the evil to be vicious and ruthless. They'll strike again; in their disappointment and failure they'll try to do as much damage as they can.' He put his arm about her shoulders. 'I hate to say all that, but I'm sure it's true.'

'Yes,' Felicity said. 'It's undoubtedly true. Do you know how they might strike?'

'Oh, at the convention,' Dawlish answered. 'I don't think there's any doubt about that.' His eyes lit up. 'So the quicker I'm back there, the better!' He squeezed her shoulders again adding: 'The one way to head it off would be to find out why Catherine Lee was in such danger; why the Pentecost girls were slaughtered; the real reason why Gerald Lee was killed.' Now his smile was gentle. 'I'm sorry, sweet, I know some of these names mean nothing to you, I'm really thinking aloud.'

'If only I could help,' Felicity said, almost desperately.

'There's one way you can help a great deal,' Dawlish told her, and she became eagerly expectant. 'You can advise me how to handle the situation between Gordon Scott and Catherine Lee.'

They sat down, their backs to the view, and he told her what had happened, making the dilemma of Gordon Scott as vivid as could be. And as he talked he thought more and more deeply about Catherine; and about the attack in which her brother had been kicked to death.

He could not clear his mind of the fact that although two of the murderers had been caught, two were still free.

CHAPTER NINETEEN

ERUPTION

Every newspaper, every radio and television channel, carried the news of Lord Elderwater's suicide; edition after edition carried stories which Dawlish and the Yard officials approved for publication. Most came from the investigation into the *Globe*'s activities in Britain and the associated groups about the world. Time and time again leading articles, secretly written or sponsored by the *Globe*, were printed in *Student Action* in parts of the world where their origin could not be easily traced. All incited rebellion and revolt. All approved the use of violence and of rifles and revolvers, flame-bombs and high explosives.

And as the offices of the newspapers were raided, all over the world, overwhelming evidence was found of the *Globe*'s part in providing funds, in making weapons available, in sending trained agitators to university after university.

In capital city after capital city, nests of revolutionaries were discovered, with plans already near completion of take-over—first at town and city level, then at national level and every move was to have been made under the cloak of *Student Action* and the need to banish the acting authorities who had failed to put the revolts down.

Arrest followed arrest. Supplies of money and arms were cut off from the rebels in the universities. In some cases, the rebels simply gave way, but all over the world there came eruptions of such violence that earlier revolts paled into insignificance.

In Paraguay, a university was burned down with half of the faculty trapped within. In two southern states of America, colleges were blown up with high explosives which took a huge toll of lives. In a Moscow suburb a group of students locked themselves into a university building and were burned alive when the army attacked. In Canada, students raided a military camp, stole tanks and armoured cars and ran amok through the nearby town, killing and maiming. In New South Wales, Australia, students set fire to a newly-built university and the fire tore through nearby homes and out to the forests, until thousands of square miles were burned out and everything living destroyed or suffocated. In Saigon, a university built with U.S. aid was blown up, resulting in a horror greater than anything in the Vietnam war. Rumours came out of China of mass revolts put down only by the ruthless use of armed force. In the north of England, hundreds of students in stolen trucks and armoured cars broke into one of the nuclear development plants and hurled high explosives and petrol bombs; only the unbelievable heroism of a few security men and the laboratory and maintenance staff saved the destruction of plant which would have spread the desolation of atomic radiation throughout the British Isles.

Everywhere, the eruptions came.

Everywhere they began in the same way—with students losing control, being inflamed to hate campaigns, orderly demonstrations turned into a rabble. Everywhere the purpose was all too clear: to break down authority, to create conditions of anarchy everywhere, ready for a take-over.

Before Elderwater's death, groups in most cities were standing by to 'restore order' and to gain control. Plan after plan was discovered, showing that first the university authorities were to be overwhelmed, then the students were to turn out local civic authorities, turning riots into full-blooded revolutions. Given a few more weeks in which to prepare, the governments of many nations would surely have fallen and the *Globe* commissars taken over. Raids on armouries, supply dumps and airfields were planned, to hamper military and police intervention.

All of these things crowded into Dawlish's mind as he prepared for and then started out on the flight back to Golana ... but this time he was not the only policeman on board. It was a charter plane, carrying delegates and advisers from most of the western European countries. In all, there were forty-seven top policemen on board, among them Van Woelden of Holland. Security police and army bomb disposal squads were checking the aircraft to make sure there was no possibility of sabotage. A tight security cordon was flung round the airport and the aircraft itself. The main runway was cleared of stand-by aircraft at the take-off.

Sitting next to Dawlish was Van Woelden, a broad-shouldered, grey-bearded man with horn-rimmed glasses. His voice was deep, at times guttural, and his English word perfect. He and Dawlish had worked together behind the Nazi lines during the war, when Van Woelden had been one of the leaders of the Dutch resistance movement.

They watched the houses and the roads getting smaller and smaller, and when at last they sat back, the Dutchman said:

'You know, don't you, that you will never be properly honoured for what you have done.'

'My job?' asked Dawlish almost vaguely. He kept thinking about Felicity and her simple advice about Gordon Scott, and he only heard what Van Woelden said with part of his mind.

'Perhaps it *was* your job,' Van Woelden replied. 'I sometimes wonder whether we know what we are put on this planet to do.' When he saw how that remark startled Dawlish, he went on: 'If you had not agitated for this conference and so precipitated action, we might not have prevented world revolution.'

'Oh stuff,' exclaimed Dawlish, uneasily.

'And nonsense, no doubt,' said Van Woelden drily. 'I can't believe it would have succeeded, Patrick, but I think there would have been pitched battles in the streets and the cities. A holocaust. Every new piece of evidence adds to my conviction. I only wish I could make sure this was recognised.'

'I only wish I knew how to make sure we don't have trouble at Gola,' Dawlish said.

'Patrick,' the Dutchman said. 'You know whom they will hate, don't you?'

'I know,' said Dawlish.

'That is another thing I was going to ask, and please, don't be offended or brush the suggestion aside. Will you have a bodyguard wherever you go, Patrick? Not just one or two men keeping an eye open for trouble, but a strong bodyguard which can really protect you.'

Dawlish smiled grimly.

'You mean, on the food-taster principle. Let the bodyguards take the first bullets.'

After a few moments Van Woelden took off his glasses, rubbed his pale, tired-looking eyes, and said quietly:

'The royal food-taster's life was considered less important

146

than the king's. You are a very great policeman, and you can be of inestimable service to society. You take frightening and formidable risks in emergency and there is no way of preventing this. I am not even sure one should attempt to prevent it. I am quite sure that you should take every possible precaution against anticipated risks.' He paused again and then went on even more soberly: 'If we asked for volunteers on this aircraft to act as your bodyguard, you would be astonished at how many would come forward.'

Quick as a flash, Dawlish retorted: 'I'd volunteer as food-taster for you, too! That's no criterion. Let me ponder, will you?'

'You are the most obstinate of men,' Van Woelden said, shrugging. He put on his glasses and his eyes became much brighter.

At each stop, more delegates entered the aircraft. From Spain, Italy, Yugoslavia, Algeria, Tunisia and Libya; from Cairo and from Beirut, from Israel and from Jordan. From Cairo, the flight would be non-stop to Gola. And each brought reports of fresh outbreaks of student violence but also news that much unrest had quietened and many feared eruptions had not taken place.

Dawlish looked out of the window as the plane swayed in its descent, and saw the university buildings, as good as new. A few workmen appeared to be putting on the finishing touches. Fires were seen to be alight under great open ovens. Mosquito nets lay over huge piles of fruit and vegetables, barrels of water, beer and wine.

'It looks more like a preparation for a fiesta,' said Hartelan of Spain.

'Perhaps it is a kind of celebration,' suggested Nielsen of Stockholm. 'A celebration of victory in advance!'

'A kind of victory,' Dawlish temporised.

At last they landed. M'gobo and his two lieutenants were there to welcome them, flags flew, bands played, people cheered, cars were waiting to take them to their rooms at the university. All along the road there were flag-waving, cheering people. Many carried roughly printed banners of welcome and many more waved those with *Welcome Dawlish* scrawled across them. When they drew within sight of the buildings,

147

Van Woelden spoke again.

'It is a celebration, Patrick. You are getting a reward of a kind.'

'Nice thought,' said Dawlish.

A policeman in a skirted uniform opened the door. Dawlish stepped out and saw Gordon Scott and Catherine, smiling their welcome, with Camilla Felista just behind them, wearing a dress of scarlet braided with gold and black and green. It was as they shook hands, and Dawlish saw the glow in Catherine's eyes, that two things clicked into place in Dawlish's mind.

'Darling, you must leave it to them to work out. You can't, you mustn't interfere, whatever you do. Gordon has to make up his mind, and if you push him in any direction, he'll probably go. He hero-worships you. But don't push, don't show any preference for Dodie or for Catherine. Leave it to Gordon, whatever you do.'

Seeing Catherine and Gordon there, he knew that Felicity was wholly right.

He 'saw' something else: the picture which had been drawn for him several times, but which he had never seen vividly until now. In the flash, there was Catherine walking between her brother, so soon to die, and her boy-friend Archie Nemaker. Dawlish had seen photographs of Nemaker, but not seen the man in the flesh. Now he could see him, and the three lovely Pentecost girls, being accosted; and Gerald going to their rescue but Nemaker walking on to the amphitheatre. 'If there's trouble,' he had said, 'I want to be in it.'

These pictures faded in the brief excitement of meeting. Then M'gobo's men and the staff of the motel section took the delegates to their quarters. Interpreters, distinguished by a purple flash on each shoulder, moved about to offer help. Each delegate was given a brochure and an agenda—drawn up by Gordon and Camilla, after brief consultations with Dawlish by telephone. Gordon was deeply involved with delegates. Camilla, always eager, began to talk.

'The Golanans are being very helpful, Mr. Dawlish—helpful and efficient. I have already the help of a staff of young men and women and I took the liberty of saying we would make payment of their salaries. There is sufficient room in the main lecture hall for the general sessions—but come, I show you.'

She took it for granted that Catherine would come with them.

There was the theatre, or lecture hall, made of pale brown wood, the well of the theatre shallow, the platform with a screen for slides or cine film, with curtains for theatrical shows. There were dressing-rooms which could be used for small committees, rehearsal rooms where larger groups would meet before or after the main sessions. And there was a communications room, very like that in the Capitol, where they could make contact with any part of the world. At a long desk in this room three girls and three youths all of university graduate age were sorting out reports.

'Everywhere the troubles are subsiding,' Camilla reported with deep pleasure. 'And here, it is as if we had no trouble, Mr. Dawlish. I . . . Yes?' she said to one of the girls, who had a long, rather sombre face.

'You asked me to tell you when the aircraft from New York is due,' the girl said.

'So, when is it due?'

'In one hour,' the girl reported. 'On board there is Assistant Commissioner Patton of New York, Captain-Inspector Leblanc from Ottawa, Captain . . .' She went on listing the names, but Dawlish was concentrating on Catherine, who seemed to catch her breath when she heard the name Patton. She turned to him.

'I would very much like to talk to you,' she said.

'Darling, you must leave it to them to work out. You can't, you mustn't interfere, whatever you do . . .'

There was a covered seat beneath a roof of palm fronds, one of many near the swimming pool, Dawlish waited for Catherine to sit down, then sat beside her. She shifted round in her seat, to see him better.

'What is it, Cathy?' he asked.

'I hate to worry you,' said Catherine, 'but there's something I need to know. About Gordon.'

'Go on,' Dawlish said, still aware of Felicity's warning.

'I am helplessly in love with him,' she said. 'I think I would accept almost any conditions just to be with him. Sometimes I think he feels that way about me. At others, I think he isn't sure. I was with him last night when a photograph of a girl fell

149

out of his wallet. He told me she was Dodie Patton, daughter of a friend of yours in New York.'

'Yes, I know Dodie,' Dawlish admitted.

'Do you—do you know if they are committed in any way?' she asked, pleading. 'Sometimes I think he's haunted by something in his past, some kind of guilt. If he were engaged to Dodie I would understand. I would...' She closed her eyes but at the same moment forced an over-brilliant smile. 'I would let him off the hook, Pat. I really would. But I don't— *oh* God.' She broke off, her eyes filming with tears and her voice almost breaking. 'I don't want to. I don't know why I'm so much in love with him, but I am.'

She stretched out her hands and touched Dawlish. She looked so very beautiful, so young, so full of life and yet shadowed by the harshness of grief and now by the talons of doubt. She was pleading for reassurance; she wasn't really asking for the truth, but just that reassurance. He's mine, she was crying within herself. He's mine, tell me he's mine!

'Darling, you must leave it to them to work out. You can't, you mustn't interfere...'

'Catherine,' Dawlish said. 'I want to ask you a question.'

'Anything,' she said. 'Anything. If you mean am I sure...'

'Do you think you love Gordon Scott as much as Archie Nemaker loves you?' asked Dawlish, and although he tried to keep the harshness out of his voice, he could not.

Catherine snatched her hand away as if his was red-hot.

CHAPTER TWENTY

THE VOICE OF HATE

She reared away from him, her hands now at his breast, as if she were afraid of him and were fending him off. It could be simply shock, he knew; and it could be much, much more. It seemed a long time before he spoke again and this time he managed to make his voice sound normal.

'Do you?' he asked. 'Have you a double problem?'

She almost gasped: 'No!'

'Cathy,' Dawlish went on. 'What really happened that day at Mid-Cal? The day when your brother was killed?'

'Oh dear God,' she breathed. 'Dear God.'

Insistently, he pressed: 'You and your brother and Archie Nemaker were walking towards the amphitheatre, and Nemaker said there was going to be trouble, so...'

'No! Gerald said that!'

'And you wanted to turn back.'

'Yes,' she breathed. 'Yes.'

'But Archie Nemaker went on.'

'Yes, he...'

'And then the men attacked the Pentecost trio.'

'Yes, yes, I've told you. I've told Gordon a hundred times!' Her eyes were wild and her voice husky.

'Cathy,' he said. 'Why?'

'You know why! There was going to be trouble, I...'

'How did you know that?'

'It was obvious, they were all rushing towards the amphitheatre.'

'Had there been trouble before?'

'No! Not real trouble, but...'

'Had there been meetings at the amphitheatre before?'

'Yes, but...'

Dawlish actually raised his hand to silence her, held his breath for a moment and then asked with almost cruel remorselessness, for obviously she was in such distress.

'How could you be sure there was going to be trouble, if this kind of thing had happened before? Was there something different, something you and your brother and your lover ...'

'*Archie wasn't my lover!*' she cried.

'Something all three of you saw and recognised as different, warned you and Gerald and made you turn away. *Why was he killed, Cathy?*'

'No, no, no!' she almost moaned.

'You must tell me sooner or later. Why not now?' Dawlish insisted. 'Why not make it easy for yourself? Why was he killed? It wasn't simply because of the Pentecost girls, was it? There was some other reason. What was it? Tell me—*now.*'

She sat there, her eyes huge, her body tense, the tears which had filmed her eyes because of Gordon Scott still shimmering. In the distance were the sounds of cars and people, of hammering, of aircraft, but just about them was only the rustling whisper of wind through the fronds above their heads and the sibilant hiss of Catherine Lee, as she took in shallow, almost panting breaths.

'*Tell me,*' Dawlish said again, '*Tell me now.*'

'Oh dear God,' she breathed. 'He—he was backing out.'

'*Who* was backing out?'

'Gerald. Oh dear God, Gerald.'

'Backing out of the revolt at the college?'

'Yes. Yes. He—he was one of the leaders.'

'You mean, he was a paid agitator?'

'No! No, he—he was always a rebel. If you'd known Gerald you'd have known he was always a rebel, always against authority. He *hated* what they were doing. At Mid-Cal they made it almost impossible for a black student to enrol, and he hated the administration for that. So he helped Kalta and the others. He was one of the informers on the campus— no one knew he was on the Students' Committee for Action, but he attended some of their secret meetings. And—and he heard they were planning to take over the college. He knew the other members of the Students' Committee, where the money came from, what the plans were. He—he had a job to do at the amphitheatre. There were some secret police there, I—I mean police in plain clothes. He was to watch them and see what they did, if they had transistor radios. But—but he couldn't do it. He wouldn't go on. That's why they killed him. The—the

152

Pentecost girls were on the committee, too, *they* wanted to back out. That's why they were killed, it wasn't simply an attack on me. Gregory Pentecost was the key-man at Mid-Cal, the meetings were held at his house. When his wife and daughters rebelled the—the real leaders wiped them all out.'

'To prevent them from talking?'

'Yes.'

'And to prevent you from telling me or Gordon or anyone else this?'

'*Yes.*'

'And Archie Nemaker—was he one of the committee?'

'Yes,' she answered, brokenly. 'Yes. And—and that night he came he told me that they were going to kill me whatever the cost, because they couldn't be sure how much Gerald and he had told me. He came to warn me to get away, but I didn't go. I wouldn't go. I felt—I felt so guilty—guilty because I'd kept silent, guilty because I'd persuaded Gerald to give up, so really causing his death. Guilty. Oh dear God, I felt guilty because in spite of it all I fell in love, and at times was wildly happy. Do you even begin to understand?'

'I think I understand a great deal,' Dawlish said, gently. He stretched out his hands, and uncertainly she placed hers in them. 'Were you on the committee?'

'No. Never.'

'How long did you know that Gerald was an active member?'

'Only for a few days. But—but I knew, If I'd told the sheriff in the beginning if only I hadn't been so afraid...' She broke off, and closed her eyes. 'You'll have to tell Gordon, of course.'

'Yes,' answered Dawlish simply. 'Unless...'

'Unless what?'

'You would like to tell him yourself.'

She was silent for a long time, but at last she said:

'If I tell him, it will help him to make up his mind, won't it?'

'Probably,' said Dawlish. 'I should certainly think so.'

He walked with her to the edge of the swimming pool, and watched as she walked off, both sturdy and graceful. She was shorter than Dodie Patton, and thicker-set, but Gordon had a choice between two most attractive young women. '*Darling, you must leave it to them to work out.*' He saw an aircraft

153

circling overhead, and could just make out the TWA symbols on the tail. He began to move very quickly, and as he reached the parked cars a police driver came forward.

'You want car, sir?'

'Please. Can you take me to the airport?'

'At once, sir.'

As they turned into the airport enclosure the TWA plane from New York was taxi-ing towards the airport buildings; by the time he had drawn up outside the control tower, M'gobo and his team were there to welcome the newcomers. There were several policemen whom he recognised and also two newspapermen, one from the *New York Times* and one from the *Los Angeles Times*, each wearing a lapel badge marked *Press*. Then Patton appeared down the steps, looking bronzed and fit.

Just behind him was a tall young man with clear-cut, handsome features and thrusting Roman nose. His eyes were hawklike; sharp and eager. He wore a *Press* badge in his lapel, and once on the ground walked briskly and confidently towards the airport building; and he avoided Dawlish's eye. Dawlish was suddenly in the middle of a group of American delegates, policemen and F.B.I., with Patton as eager as any to see him. Patton stayed close to his side when M'gobo came forward with an official welcome. Dawlish waited until the formalities were over, then nudged Patton and at the same time whispered into M'gobo's ear.

'Can you spare me a moment, Captain M'gobo?'

'At once,' the Chief of Police replied. They turned away, as he went on: 'It is perhaps to ask me to give special consideration to your good friend Assistant Commissioner Patton...'

'I'm sure you would do that, anyhow,' said Dawlish. 'No. I would like you personally to handle the baggage of a young newspaperman—the tall man in the biscuit-coloured suit, who is waiting by the baggage ramp.'

'Young Neil, from L.A.?' asked Patton, in surprise.

'He's sometimes known as Nemaker,' Dawlish said.

They went over as the baggage came through the entry flaps and on to the circular conveyor. Policemen and Pressmen as well as porters were handling the baggage, and Neil *alias* Nemaker waited for his cases with obvious tension. He moved suddenly towards a lightweight case with yellow lines about it in the form of a cross. He lifted it, then saw another, smaller but similarly marked, and picked that up with his free hand. As he did so, M'gobo took one from him and Dawlish the other. Appalled, Nemaker spun round—to find Patton blocking his path. He swung round again and made a wild rush, attempting to jump over the conveyor, but caught his foot on a metal rung, tripped and fell. One glance inside one case was enough to show that he had come here to destroy them all.

By the time the news of his arrest was broadcast round the world, all but a few remnants of the powers that had driven *Student Action* to its near disastrous end were caught. Reports came in to the delegates from country after country, and each of them went through Camilla's hands and lodged immovably in her computer mind.

At half-past nine next morning the theatre was crowded, hardly a seat was empty. The Press gallery, above the main auditorium, was as crowded. The flag of every nation represented hung from the walls. The Golana police in dress uniforms of bright green stood at attention as the President came in, flanked by his ministers. A burst of cheering resounded before he said with great simplicity:

'We are trying to make a model nation. We welcome you in your work to enable us to live in a world not only at peace but free from crime.'

Van Woelden, in the chair, led the applause; and said as simply that they were here with great hope—and then added that but for Deputy Assistant Commissioner Dawlish they might not be here at all. He called on M'gobo to say why, and M'gobo, a little laboured because he was so self-conscious, said:

'First, I tell you I am the proudest man in this world tonight. To have the greatest detectives, the greatest policemen from each nation here as my guest—I tell you it is almost too much for me.' Indeed for a moment it seemed as if he would not be able to go on, he was so tense with emotion. But he fought for a calm voice and found it.

'I also wish to pay tribute to Deputy Assistant Commissioner Dawlish. I want to tell you...' And he told them clearly and precisely how Dawlish had worked and warned him about Nemaker. 'And, Mr. Chairman, Mr. President and distinguished delegates, I am to tell you that in Nemaker's baggage there was enough high explosive to kill us all in this room.'

There was silence; utter silence.

Then, Van Woelden rose and beckoned Dawlish to stand.

And as he rose there was a thunder of applause which went on and on; with Camilla Felista waving and shouting, and Gordon Scott and Cathy in the back of the theatre, Scott cheering, Cathy crying and yet laughing at the same time.

For two days, the conference dealt with the student revolts, taking report after report; and each one showed how near the final explosion the youth of the world had been. On the third day, very warm outside but beautifully cool in the theatre, Van Woelden opened the meeting with characteristic directness.

'The main business has been concluded, and there can be few among us who have not realised the danger we were in. And such danger can come upon us again, without warning. We are not fools enough to believe that the future is easy: the war against crime will become fiercer and fiercer, everywhere.

'We need—we who are delegates from our nations need—a framework in which to speed the process of detection, to traverse the world as fast as criminals can, to be at the places they come to almost before they arrive. To do this we need a secretariat. We need a permanent staff. We need a base from which we can operate. Today and tomorrow, we shall debate these needs, and how best we can satisfy them.' And he went on: 'Already with Camilla Felista, we have a remarkable administrator. I do declare there is not a face among you which she could not describe down to the smallest mole. She is a woman in a million.'

As they applauded, Camilla blushed and bowed.

Then Van Woelden went on: 'I am also going to ask the conference to request the British authorities to release Mr. Dawlish from his duties in Britain to become the permanent chairman...'

Randy Patton sprang up.

'I want to second that!' he cried.

There was a roar of applause that never seemed to stop. But it did at last.

'Camilla,' said Dawlish. 'I don't know what I shall be able to do but certainly I can help to get the secretariat started. And for the time being you can work from here.'

'Here, or anywhere, I will work,' Camilla said fiercely. 'At last I am consummated, my life is truly fulfilled.'

'Gordon,' said Randy Patton, about the same time but in another room. 'I would have had to be blind not to notice you avoided me when you could. Don't be that way, son. What there is between you and Dodie is between you two, not me. The only thing I ask is that if you want to break with Dodie, you take the first chance you can to tell her so yourself.'

'Cathy,' Gordon Scott said, 'I know it must sound incredible, but I *was* in love with Dodie, and sometimes I feel such a heel about her that I wonder whether I still am, in a way. But I tell you I have *never* felt for her or for anybody the way I feel towards you.'

'Gordon,' Cathy said, quite steadily. 'I think you should go and see her again, as soon as you can. And when you've seen her, you will really be sure how you feel.'

'Darling,' said Dawlish to Felicity, soon after he got home, 'don't have any doubt about this: if you'd rather I stayed in Britain and went on doing what I'm doing, then that's exactly what I'll do.'

'The one thing you have to do is what you think is right,' said Felicity, and laughed. 'As if you didn't know!'

A SELECTION OF FINE READING AVAILABLE IN CORGI BOOKS

A SELECTION OF FINE READING AVAILABLE IN CORGI BOOKS

War (contd.)

☐ 552 08874 9   **SS GENERAL**   *Sven Hassel* 35p
☐ 552 09178 2   **REIGN OF HELL**   *Sven Hassel* 35p
☐ 552 09144 8   **THE STRAITS OF MESSINA**   *Johannes Steinhoff* 40p
☐ 552 08986 9   **DUEL OF EAGLES** (illustrated)   *Peter Townsend* 50p
☐ 552 09092 1   **WEREWOLF**   *Charles Whiting* 35p
☐ 552 09222 3   **BEYOND THE TUMULT** (illustrated)   *Barry Winchester* 40p

Romance

☐ 552 09198 7   **A HOUSE FOR SISTER MARY**   *Lucilla Andrews* 30p
☐ 552 09207 X   **THE GREEN EMPRESS**   *Elizabeth Cadell* 30p
☐ 552 09208 8   **BRIDAL ARRAY**   *Elizabeth Cadell* 30p
☐ 552 09228 2   **THE SEVEN SLEEPERS**   *Kate Norway* 30p

Science Fiction

☐ 552 09184 7   **SATAN'S WORLD**   *Poaul Anderson* 35p
☐ 552 09229 0   **STAR TREK 7**   *James Blish* 30p
☐ 552 09167 7   **THE ALIEN WAY**   *Gordon R. Dickson* 30p
☐ 552 09149 9   **STURGEON IN ORBIT**   *Theodore Sturgeon* 30p

General

☐ 552 09100 6   **FANNY HILL'S COOKBOOK**   *L. H. Braun & W. Adams* 40p
☐ 552 08926 5   **S IS FOR SEX**   *Robert Chartham* 50p
☐ 552 09151 0   **THE DRAGON AND THE PHOENIX**   *Eric Chou* 50p
☐ 552 98958 4   **THE ISLAND RACE Vol. 1**   *Winston S. Churchill* 125p
☐ 552 98959 5   **THE ISLAND RACE Vol. 2**   *Winston S. Churchill* 125p
☐ 552 08800 5   **CHARIOTS OF THE GODS** (illustrated)   *Erich von Daniken* 35p
☐ 552 09073 2   **RETURN TO THE STARS** (illustrated)   *Erich von Daniken* 40p
☐ 552 09135 9   **THE HUMAN ANIMAL** (illustrated)   *Hans Hass* 40p
☐ 552 07400 4   **MY LIFE AND LOVES**   *Frank Harris* 65p
☐ 552 98744 4   **MAKING LOVE** (Photographs)   *Walter Hartford* 85p
☐ 552 08992 3   **MASTERING WITCHCRAFT**   *Paul Huson* 35p
☐ 552 09062 X   **THE SENSUOUS MAN**   *'M'* 35p
☐ 552 08069 1   **THE OTHER VICTORIANS**   *Steven Marcus* 50p
☐ 552 09116 2   **A BRITISH SURVEY IN FEMALE SEXUALITY**
                                                            Sandra McDermott 40p
☐ 552 09230 4   **BUGLES AND A TIGER**   *John Masters* 40p
☐ 552 08010 1   **THE NAKED APE**   *Desmond Morris* 30p
☐ 552 09016 6   **GOLF TACTICS**   *Arnold Palmer* 45p
☐ 552 09232 0   **SECRET OF THE ANDES**   *Brother Philip* 30p
☐ 552 09231 2   **NUNAGA** (illustrated)   *Duncan Pryde* 45p
☐ 552 08880 3   **THE THIRTEENTH CANDLE**   *T. Lobsang Rampa* 25p

A SELECTION OF FINE READING AVAILABLE IN CORGI BOOKS

General (*contd.*)

☐ 552 09044 1 SEX ENERGY   *Robert S. de Ropp* 35p
☐ 552 09145 6 THE NYMPHO AND OTHER MANIACS   *Irving Wallace* 40p

Western

☐ 552 09147 2 IN THE DAYS OF VICTORIO (illustrated)   *Eve Ball* 40p
☐ 552 09095 6 APACHE   *Will Levington Comfort* 30p
☐ 552 09170 7 SUDDEN—DEAD OR ALIVE   *Frederick H. Christian* 30p
☐ 552 09113 8 TWO MILES TO THE BORDER No. 70   *J. T. Edson* 25p
☐ 552 08288 0 No. 50 GOODNIGHT'S DREAM   *J. T. Edson* 25p
☐ 552 09227 4 YOU'RE IN COMMAND NOW, MR. FOG No. 71
                                                              J. T. Edson 30p
☐ 552 09112 X THE DAYBREAKERS   *Louis L'Amour* 25p
☐ 552 09191 X TREASURE MOUNTAIN   *Louis L'Amour* 30p
☐ 552 09098 0 PAINTED PONIES   *Alan Le May* 35p
☐ 552 09165 0 THE GALLOWS EXPRESS No. 19   *Louis Masterson* 25p
☐ 552 09097 2 VALLEY OF THE SHADOW   *Charles Marquis Warren* 35p

Crime

☐ 552 09224 X ALIAS THE BARON   *John Creasey* 30p
☐ 552 09225 8 MYSTERY MOTIVE   *John Creasey* 30p
☐ 552 09073 5 INNOCENT BYSTANDERS   *James Munro* 30p
☐ 552 09204 5 THE EXECUTIONER: MIAMI MASSACRE   *Don Pendleton* 30p
☐ 552 09205 3 THE EXECUTIONER: ASSAULT ON SOHO
                                                          Don Pendleton 30p
☐ 552 09206 1 THE EXECUTIONER: NIGHTMARE IN NEW YORK
                                                          Don Pendleton 30p
☐ 552 09111 1 THE ERECTION SET   *Mickey Spillane* 40p
☐ 552 09056 5 SHAFT   *Ernest Tidyman* 30p
☐ 552 09072 7 SHAFT'S BIG SCORE   *Ernest Tidyman* 30p

All these books are available at your bookshop or newsagent: or can be ordered direct from the publisher. Just tick the titles you want and fill in the form below.

CORGI BOOKS, Cash Sales Department, P.O. Box 11, Falmouth, Cornwall.
Please send cheque or postal order. No currency, and allow 6p per book to cover the cost of postage and packing in the U.K. and overseas.

NAME ....

ADDRESS ....

(MAY 73) ....